Cherry Street

Made to Kill

David Michael Campo

PublishAmerica
Baltimore

© 2010 by David Michael Campo.
All rights reserved. No part of this book may be reproduced, stored in a retrieval system or transmitted in any form or by any means without the prior written permission of the publishers, except by a reviewer who may quote brief passages in a review to be printed in a newspaper, magazine or journal.

First printing

All characters in this book are fictitious, and any resemblance to real persons, living or dead, is coincidental.

PublishAmerica has allowed this work to remain exactly as the author intended, verbatim, without editorial input.

Hardcover 978-1-4489-3101-9
Softcover 978-1-4489-4080-6
PUBLISHED BY PUBLISHAMERICA, LLLP
www.publishamerica.com
Baltimore

Printed in the United States of America

To Heather
is your Husband Safe?

David Camp

Dedication

I would like to dedicate this book to my wife, Angela, my three children, Carrie, Adam, and Troy. Without their support, this book would have not been possible.

To whom it may concern:

I have taken pen in hand to tell you the story of my life. The life of a man, whom with and without the permission of his own government, committed crimes against his fellow man and countrymen. Crimes on a level that can only be appreciated by reading the manuscript provided. I am neither proud nor ashamed of my life. It is what it is. I have not embellished the facts because they need not be embellished. I feel it is important that the citizens of this country be aware of the things that go on behind closed doors sanctioned by their own government. To have the courage to investigate and report what you have learned. Keep in mind my life is not an isolated case. People like me *do* exist. We always have, and probably always will.

CHAPTER ONE

It was a beautiful day, the day of my birth, May 22, 1946. I was born into a small German community in Southern Illinois. My mother was of good German stock, maiden name Lidzenbrau. My father on the other hand was pure Italian, the son of a poor working class family from Cicely. My grandfather was a boot maker, proud but poor.

My father came to the United States when he was eighteen years old. Boot making was not his profession of choice. He wanted more than that of a poor working man. So he set off on the adventure of a life time. The date was June 6th, 1931, the weather was fair, it was an uneventful day except for the fact he was leaving his home, his country, and everyone he knew for an uncertain life in America.

Landing on Ellis Island some weeks later he saw Lady Liberty for the first time. He was processed at Ellis Island with my Great Uncle Salvador Campanalia as his sponsor. Salvador is my father's uncle on my grandfather's side. My father's name was Michael Alphonso Campanalia. While living with Uncle Sal, he found a job on the docks. It was hard work and not much pay, but never the less he was grateful to have a job. In his spare time he would hang out at the local gym doing a little light boxing. One day, the manager asked my father if he would like to box for money. My father replied, "How much?" The man told him "Twenty dollars if you lose, sixty if you win." (Sixty dollars was more than a week's earnings in 1932.) My father did not want to be a boxer; he wanted to be a land owner, a farmer. The boxing promoter for the gym, Mr. Rockford told the manager Mr. Carbone, that my father needed a boxers name and Campanalia was not it. After some discussion they came up with Michael Carson. It sounded more American than Michael Alphonso Campanolia. He trained as hard as he could when he was not working his shift at the docks. Mike was a lean five foot eleven inches, one hundred and seventy-five pounds, and hungry. Hungry for more than the life of a dock hand.

One Saturday night that May, the newly named boxer was as scared as he was anxious. It was his first fight. How would he do? Would he last as long as he was expected to last? His mind was racing, so many questions and so much pressure. He stepped into the ring with a veteran fighter, Sammy "The Sleeper" Fitzgerald. They called him Sammy "The Sleeper" because he had knocked so many people out in his career. The bell sounded and it was the beginning of round one. Half scared and half sick from worry, the two touched gloves and came out fighting. Sammy came across with a left jab, and then a right cross. My father blocked the right cross and countered with a right cross. That was it; there would be no round two. Twenty-Six seconds into the first round, Mike Carson knocked Sammy "The Sleeper" Fitzgerald out cold! The crowd was stunned. People could be heard mumbling to one another, "Who is this kid?" and "Where did he come from?" My father cost a lot of money to a lot of people. Nobody was betting on him, well almost nobody. My Great Uncle Sal bet five dollars. The odds were six to one in favor of Sammy "The Sleeper". Uncle Sal almost passed out at the sight of his winnings, six days pay. Mr. Carbone as well as Mr. Rockford were upset at first with the result of the fight. They, like everyone else expected my father to lose. It did not take them long to figure out they had a potential gold mine on their hands with my dad, as long as what just happened was not a fluke. My father quit his job and began full time training. No more dock work for Mike Carson.

At the age of nineteen he was off on another unsure adventure. Without a job and only the hope of making it big, Uncle Sal told him he believed in him, and that he had potential. This was a hope that was shared by so many who came before my father. Mr. Rockford paid him Fifteen dollars a week to train in addition to covering all expenses for training. He was told when he fought again he would be paid thirty-five percent and the remaining sixty-five percent would go to Mr. Rockford. This seemed like a good deal to a Nineteen year old immigrant from Italy who spoke broken English.

After three months of training day in and day out, it was time to see if Michael Carson had what it takes to pull off another victory. This time he was matched up against a veteran fighter named Carl Killwolski, or "Killer Killwolski" as they called him. My father wondered if the press would ever give him a solid ring name now that he was a boxer. This is something all fighters want. The purse on this fight was five hundred dollars to the winner and one hundred fifty dollars for the loser.

September 2nd, 1932 came around and my father had trimmed down to one hundred and sixty-eight pounds. His opponent was equally matched at five foot ten inches, one hundred seventy-one pounds and twenty three years old. The two fighters sized each other up. Round one began by both men trading blows. It was an uneventful round. During round two my father took an upper cut to the chin, he staggered back, if not for the ropes he would have gone down. My Uncle Sal must have panicked at the thought of losing the ten dollars he bet, this time the odds were five to one. Michael Carson came back off the ropes with a immediate right cross, just two minutes and fifteen seconds into the second round, there for everybody to see, "Killer Killwolski" was on his back, out cold! The crowd cheered! Even those who had lost money tipped their hats to Michael Carson.

The next day the paper read Michael "The Mauler" Carson takes out "Killer Killwolski" in the second round. My father was walking on air. His name was in the paper and he had been given a boxing nickname that did not sound bad, not bad at all. His manager Mr. Carbone told him "You did okay, don't get cocky, you made plenty of mistakes".

He said to take tomorrow off then be back at the gym on Monday, we have a lot of work to do. I guess that let the wind out of his sails, but he knew he needed the reality check. He knew he needed a lot of work, so on Monday back to the gym it was. Mr. Carbone told him "The fight was won on half luck and half talent". "Let's concentrate on building your talent" he said. He trained, he fought, and he won. He trained, he fought, he won, and so it went. Time flew by, it was now 1935 and he had been boxing for three years. He had managed to get his own little apartment. It was not much, but he was not there much anyway. Mike was saving as much money as he could because he still wanted his own land and farm.

In early April 1935, he was ready for the fight that would put him three, maybe four, fights away from a "Title fight". If he won this fight, his take would be almost twelve thousand dollars. Mike "The Mauler" Carson had sixteen wins by knock out, two wins by decision, and one draw. Mike's next opponent was once again "Killer Killwolski". It was going to be a rematch, and they both needed to win. Uncle Sal couldn't even place money on the fight because it was too close to call. The big night came, in round one the two pounded on each other. Neither man gave an inch. By the end of round six they were both beaten bloody. Their eyes swollen with cuts in the eyebrows, both had bloody noses, yet neither would back down. Round nine came and both men were wearing each other down. My father's vision was blurred and his eyes puffy from the abuse, it was then that "killer" hit him so hard that his feet left the ground. "One, two, three, four," counted the referee. He staggered to his feet. It was will power at this point that kept him going. Two minutes and twenty-seven seconds into the ninth round my father saw an opening. He hit "killer" with everything he had left. "Killer" went down, one, two, three, four, he still didn't move five, six, seven, eight, nine, ten. It was over, he had won. "Killer's" corner people ran in the ring. My father knew something was wrong when he saw the doctor rush in amongst the others. "Killer" was dead. My father had hit him so hard that the blow to the left side of his head had killed him! My father was sick to his stomach. Sure he wanted to win, but not like this. Everyone said to it was not his fault. It was just a freak accident. However, it didn't help the way he felt.

The next day, the local papers front page reported Michael "The

Mauler" terminates "Killer Killwolski" in Nine Rounds. My father was never the same after that fight. He hung up his gloves. This upset a lot of people, the same people who were counting on him to continue making them money. What those people didn't know was what it was like to live with the guilt of having killed a man in the ring. A man with a wife and two children now left behind.

He had saved quite a bit of money, but now what would he do, where will he go from here? He was at a low point in his life.

CHAPTER TWO

Larry Burk was my father's best friend; they met while working on the docks. Larry was from a small German community in Southern Illinois. He always talked about life on the farm and how he wished he could go back. He simply did not have the money to buy land. Now he had a wife and three children in New York, and going back to the farm was no longer an option. They were talking one day and he told my father that his Uncle Jacob Lidzenbrau was selling his farm and moving to town to retire. It sounded perfect! Three hundred and twenty acres of farm land far away from the memory of the boxing ring. So, his friend Larry contacted his uncle and said that his friend Michael was going to come see him about buying the farm. He was once again Michael Alphonso Campanalia, Michael "The Mauler" Carson was just a memory. Now on another adventure, he was heading to Waterloo, Illinois to see about being a farmer.

It was July 2, 1935 and my father arrived in the small town of Waterloo Illinois. This was a long trip from New York, but he was there and he liked the look of the area. It was definitely a rural farming community. After asking around town for directions to Jacob Lidzenbrau's farm and encountering a lot of strange looks. This was probably because of the accent he had; he was on the last leg of his journey to Jacob's farm.

The house was located about twenty-five or thirty minutes out of town, rock roads all the way. When he pulled in he saw a two story farm house, a very large barn, a lake, gardens, a fruit orchard, and a variety of farm animals. He was taken aback by all of it, he was sold. Now if he could get Jacob to agree. He pulled up to the house and he was greeted almost before he got out of his car.

Jacob Lidzenbrau was a large man. He stood six feet two inches, weighed two hundred forty to two hundred fifty pounds, and was sixty-five years old. Jacob had very large hands, so large that when they shook hands my father's hand almost disappeared. He had gray hair and dark skin from life in the outdoors. His skin was hard and leather like. There were many wrinkles from the years of labor in the sun. His voice was deep and strong, but his tone was gentle and kind. It was 11:30am and they were getting ready to sit down to have dinner. "You will join us, so we will talk about what you came here for." As they approached the back door they were greeted by his wife Elizabeth. She was a small German woman who has spent her whole life on the farm. She was what you would call the salt of the earth, a wonderful person by any standards. She led them to the kitchen where she was preparing to serve dinner. They had cheese and crackers, homemade bread, ham steak, fresh green beans, corn on the cob, and canned peaches for dessert. They talked for a while and got to know each other.

Jacob wanted to not only make sure my father could afford to buy the farm; he also wanted to make sure he wanted to sell it to him. They walked the entire farm that day and they talked for hours. They finally agreed on a price of thirty-seven thousand dollars. This was a lot of money, but my father had a little more than enough. They shook hands and my father said he was going back to town to find a place to stay. Jacob said, "No you will stay here". "It is your farm now and you will stay here until I move, this way I can help you get settled into this life". My father agreed.

July 4th was a big day for the Lidzenbrau family. The entire family at large showed up at Jacob's house for a family gathering that morning. They ate breakfast, tended to the livestock, and started getting ready for the family gathering. The tables were set and Jacob started the fire pit. He put a young pig on the spick for the family's dinner. The family started to trickle in at 10:30am and by 1:00pm there must have been sixty or more Lidzenbrau and extended family members there. There were horseshoe pits for the men, baseball for the kids, all while the women worked quite hard to feed everyone and tend to the children. Everyone was having a good time. Then, from nowhere, my father spotted a young lady. He was absolutely taken back by her beauty. She was five foot six inches tall, had long brown hair, blue eyes, and weighed about one hundred ten pounds. He could not stop starring at her. She spotted him and smiled. She then turned away and went back to serve the children food. Well, Jacob told him "It is not polite to stare and that is my great niece Christine Lidzenbrau, and no she is not married nor is she attached to anyone. She is only nineteen years old. Would you like to meet her" he asked. "Of course" my father replied. We will have to go through her father, my nephew Charlie. Mind your tongue and let me talk, that's the way it is done around here. Jacob introduced my father to Charlie and they exchanged pleasantries for a few minutes. Jacob asked, "How's the wife and children doing?" and "How's Christine?" "I thought she would be married by now." I know, muttered Charlie. She is a beautiful girl, but she is somewhat of a free spirited person and a lot of men do not like that in a woman. "Well if it's ok with you Charlie and only if it is ok with you, I would like to introduce young Michael to your daughter Christine, but only with your permission of course." Charlie already knew who my father was. He knew about the boxing and that he just bought Jacob's farm by paying cash. He seemed to like my father and the fact that he was on his third bucket of beer did not hurt. "Well Jacob, if you say he is ok then that is good enough for me, but you make sure he understands how it works, she is my baby girl."

"I'll explain everything to him," remarked Jacob. Jacob then led my father over to meet Christine. She was stand offish at first and she did not seem too receptive. They talked for awhile and then took a walk, but not too far since they were being watched. My father asked if he could call on her. She told him it was ok with her but he would have to ask for her father's permission. With all the courage any young man could muster up, my father went to Charlie and asked if it would be ok to call on his daughter. Charlie sized him up and down then told him to come by for supper next Saturday night at five o'clock sharp, and we will see how it goes.

They courted for three months under supervision and then finally they were allowed to be out alone. After eight months from the first date, my father asked my mother to marry him. Of course she said yes. They married September of 1936.

After three years of marriage they had a daughter born in October 1939. Her name was Debra Elizabeth Campanalia. As she grew my father said she favored the Italian side of her family and would be a heart breaker some day.

Yet again in September of 1942, my mother gave birth to my older brother whom was named after his best friend, Larry Burk, whom he said without he would have never met my mother. He named my brother Lawrence Craig Campanalia. My brother did not like the name Lawrence, so everyone calls him Craig. That is unless I was trying to irritate him.

On May 22, 1946, I was born. They named me, David Michael Campanalia. I definitely favored my father. You could not tell I had a mother of German decent.

Then finally, one more time in January of 1948, my mother gave birth to my younger brothers, "The Twins" Terry Lee Campanalia and Todd Leon Campanalia. They favored my mother's side of the family. They had fair skinned with lighter colored hair. Mom and dad always said the twins were a hand full, "Double Trouble".

Life on the farm was always wonderful for me. I could hunt, fish, and there was always something to do. Of course, there were always chores to do. There was always work to be done and it never stopped, but I did not mind at all. My father was not much of a crop farmer. He preferred to raise livestock. We had anywhere between one hundred thirty to one hundred fifty head of cattle at any given time. There always were some hogs for eating and few to sell from time to time. We had chickens for eggs and for eating. My mother canned a lot of fruits and vegetables from the orchards and the gardens. Ducks and geese were kept on the pond. It was the life, living on the farm. I was very close to my father. I enjoyed hunting and fishing with him or just "hanging out." He taught all of us boys to box. It was important to learn to defend ourselves he told us. By the time I was twelve I could beat my older brother Craig in a boxing match. Mom said of all my boys you look the most like your father and my father told me of all of the boys I had the gift of boxing. I never boxed anyone except my brother and my father and that was for fun. There were a few fights in school that I was in. It seemed that I also inherited my mother's temper. Like I said, I was happy on the farm; that was until my father died.

    A blood vessel burst in his head while at the kitchen table reading the paper. I was fourteen years old, it was August 1960. I thought my life had ended. After that things changed. I was constantly fighting at school or any other place I could pick a fight. I had a chip on my shoulder and I could not shake it.

    It had been just over one year since my father's death when my mother started seeing another man. His name was Wayne Seinlieng. A large man he was in weight as well as height. I did not care for him partially because he was not my father and partially because I just did not like him as a person. Wayne was a big time farmer from one of the older established families in the community whom my mother had known since grade school. He too was a widower and had no children of his own. My mother and Wayne dated for some time and then married when I was seventeen. By now my brother Craig had joined the Army and was on his way to Vietnam. My sister was married and she moved to St. Louis, Missouri. It was just my two little brothers and I left at home. As for me, I was still fighting a lot and always in some sort of trouble. My stepfather and I did not get along. We butted heads almost daily. He told me that I reminded him of my father more than once that actually made me proud. My stepfather as time went by became abusive towards us but mostly to my mother. This was especially true when he drank. One day we were fighting over a chore I had done not to his liking. I stood my ground, after all I was eighteen years old and I was not scared of him despite his large size. Things started to get ugly when my mother stepped in trying to protect me, and that's when it happened. He threw my mother to the side; she hit the kitchen wall, and then fell to the floor. He proceeded to hit me several times. I was able to get out of the kitchen. I ran outside and at that moment all I knew was that I wanted him to die!

I went to his truck opened the glove box where he kept a stud nose 38 pistol. After looking at it I took it, and went back into the house in the kitchen and saw that he and my mother were still fighting. I called his name, he turned and I shot him in the chest. The fat bastard fell hard. I walked over to him lying on the floor, still alive and put two more bullets into his head. My mother was in shock. She was screaming hysterically "Why, Why, Why?" and "How could you do this?" All I knew was I had to get out of there. I was not going to wait for the police to arrive to sort this out. I went outside hopped into his truck and drove off. Not sure where to go, I just drove. I headed toward St. Louis, driving his truck downtown until I found a place to park out of the way where I would not be spotted. Once I parked I went through the truck to see what I could find. I found a box of bullets for the .38 and an envelope marked cattle sale. I opened it and there was thirteen thousand eight hundred dollars. No question about it, I took the money and the shells and I left the truck. I needed to get away from that truck and out of the area fast.

Quickly, I started walking. Within a few blocks I came upon a clothing store where there I bought some new clothes. I bought a couple pairs of jeans; a few button up shirts, a pair of sneakers, some underwear, and a back pack. I then changed clothes at the store and threw my old clothes away.

After heading back down the street and walking a few more blocks I came upon Union Station Train Depot. I went inside and bought a ticket to Kansas City, Missouri. One hour fifteen minutes later I was on the train and out of the area. That was a long hour and fifteen minutes. From the time I killed my stepfather till I boarded the train had been about four and half hours.

Later that evening I was in Kansas City, Missouri. I found a diner and grabbed myself some food. I then went around the back of the dinner, curled up in a pile of empty boxes, and went to sleep. I did not sleep very well that night and woke up the next morning cold and hungry. I went back into the diner and bought myself something to eat. After eating my meal I started back down the road.

    I walked a few miles when I came upon on a truck stop. I went inside to use the restroom. I bought myself a blue jean jacket and a Coke from the store. I walked outside not sure what to do or where to go. An old trucker asked me, "Where you headed boy?" I responded, "I do not know, anywhere but here." He told me he could use some company if I wanted to go to Chicago. "What the hell sounds good to me," I replied. The next thing I knew I was getting into a big rig and heading for Chicago Illinois. He was a friendly pleasant man who talked a lot. I just sat there and listened. We stopped that afternoon for fuel and something to eat, and then back on the open road we went. It became dark and I nodded off. I was awakened by the old trucker telling me to get up. I thought to myself, guess we were already in Chicago, but I was wrong. We were pulled over on the side of the road and the old trucker suddenly seemed different. "Wake up, are you up yet?" "Yes, I am." Well this free ride is over boy, "he exclaimed." I looked up as he put a pistol to my head as he told me "You have two choices die or suck my cock." I looked down as he had his cock out and was ready for business. I knew at eighteen years of age I did not want to die, and I knew I did not want to suck his cock. I did have a pistol of my own, but how do I get to it with no time to spare. It was tucked in the back of my pants under my jacket. I told the trucker, I would suck his cock, but I could not do it if he had a gun to my head. It made me too nervous and I did not want him to get excited, while in the moment, and accidentally pull the trigger. He pointed the gun up towards the ceiling of the truck, one problem solved. Now to get to my pistol I leaned over as if I was going to suck him off, I put my left hand on his thigh as my right hand retrieved my stud nose .38, I then slid my left hand toward his cock. I could see he was preoccupied with what he thought was about to happen and I was able to bring my right hand around, and from his lap, shot him under the chin. The bullet came out the top of his head. He was dead instantly and I was glad I killed him! He was a nasty filthy son of a bitch. I have now killed two men in two days and I have no regrets about either one of them. I took the money he had and put it in my backpack.

CHAPTER THREE

    I hit the road, stuck my thumb out and started hitchhiking towards Chicago. One hundred eighty miles the sign read. I guess I walked around two or three miles before I was given a ride. By now it was nine thirty. The young man who pulled over to give me a ride seemed nice enough. He said he was headed home, back to Chicago. The man talked a lot so, I listened. I suppose he was bored and wanted some company. He asked me where in Chicago I was going, I told him anywhere it did not matter. He asked if I had a place to stay or a job. I told him I had the clothes on my back and no other plans at the moment. We pulled over on the south side of Chicago at a gas station and I thanked him for the ride. He wished me good luck. Like I said, he was nice enough person. After that I just needed to sleep, so I found a place behind some dumpsters and curled up on some cardboard and slept like a baby until I was awakened by the sound of a trash truck coming to empty the dumpster. It was around 7:30am on day three of my new life. A life of which at this point I was not sure I would survive to make it today four.

    For the next six days I slept wherever I could. I ate at cheap diners and washed up at gas stations or in the restroom of a restaurant. I washed my clothes at laundry mats and always kept a low profile, I even grew a mustache, something my mother would not have let me do.

Even though, by sixteen I was more than capable of doing so. It was on the night of the tenth day I had found a place to sleep again behind some dumpsters in an alley. I curled up and slept on some cardboard boxes again. I had just settled in and fell asleep when around 10:30pm I was awakened by someone kicking me, and I mean kicking me hard. It was two homeless men, they were robbing me. "Give me your money, your backpack, and your watch" the one yelled at me. I told them if I had money I would not be sleeping behind this dumpster. They insisted I give up my backpack. I knew I could not afford to give up what money I had. I reached behind my coat and pulled out my pistol. I can still see that look on their faces then I shot and killed both of them, I then stole their money. Between them, they had three dollars and forty seven cents. That is all they had, three dollars and forty-seven cents. They were dead, not for money, but because they tried to rob me. Again I have killed four people in less than ten days and yet I feel no regret up to this point. The only thing I have felt is satisfaction for having killed all of them. I found another place to sleep just a few miles down the road behind yet another dumpster. It was 1:30am and again I slept like a baby until the sun came up and hit me in the face. It was time to move on.

The day started out the same, find somewhere to clean up, get a meal, and try my best to keep a low profile. Well, that is the way it started, but not the way it ended. Later that afternoon, I found myself walking through the Italian section of town. It felt good to be here. I blended in fairly well, that is until I walked down Cherry St. It was there where I was approached by two young men. They were young Italian men. One I could tell was my age. The other was older, mid twenties, and he did most of the talking. He wanted me to pay for the privilege of using his street. I told him "No problem, I will go back the way I came." By this time the younger one was standing behind me and he told me it was too late. "You are already on our street, pay-up mother fucker."

"What's in your backpack the older one barked?" Nothing, just some clothes, I am broke. I do not have anything, "Give me your Shoes," the young one said. By this time we started to draw a crowd at the car lot across the street. Older Italian men where gathering to watch the show. Same one they have seen many times before no doubt. I was not about to shoot anyone since I did not believe my life was being threatened, but I was not going to give them my shoes or anything else to these cock suckers for that matter. They were apparently used to getting away with this and to them it was just business. Not today. The younger one pushed me from behind then the older one swung at me. I ducked and came back with a right cross; I hit him with everything in my body. He hit the ground and he hit hard I turned to my left just in time to come at the younger one with an over hand punch right to the bridge of his nose. He was finished. Blood was pouring out of his nose, his vision was blurred; he could not have fought if he wanted to. He laid there on the side walk of Cherry St. bleeding and not looking so tough. His friend was not looking any better, not moving at all. I decided it was time to disappear. At this point I started to walk away. I noticed a larger older Italian man around forty approaching me. He said, "Come here boy." Then another man appeared in front of me blocking my path. I stopped and I told them, "I do not want any trouble; I just want to get out of here." The larger of the two told me, "It is too late for that. You need to come with us. Our boss wants to talk to you." He then lifted his shirt to show me he was carrying a gun. His friend did likewise. I had my gun, but did not want to go for it if I didn't have to.

    We walked straight to the car lot across the street, Tortanallia's car lot. By now, the young men I had fought where on their feet, and not happy. This does not look good for me, but still I resisted the urge to go for my pistol. They walked me into a small building around the back of the car lot. We stood there for a few minutes. It seemed much longer since no one spoke. Then the door opened, a man came in and introduced himself as "Big Tony" Tony Tortanallia and those two young men who you just beat the crap out of are with me. They are part of my "family". Now what the fuck do you think I should do, you tell me? "I thought about it for just one minute and replied," My father often said if you are going to wear a pair of man's shoes make sure you can fill them. It looks to me like they are wearing the wrong shoes." He chuckled, "you have me there. You fucked them up, but still I cannot just let it go". If I do that then it would be open season on my family.

This I cannot allow. He paused, and then said "I could make you a junior member of my family and then we just let this go as a misunderstanding." What do you say? Do you want a job or do you want to take your chances? "A job sounds good to me," I replied. Tony asked me if I was the least bit curious as to why he would even bother to offer me a job. Before I could speak the older of the two men who had escorted me to the building spoke out, he said "If he doesn't want to know, I sure as fuck would like to know why you offered him a job instead of what I think we should be doing." Tony barked back, you could tell he was not happy. He obviously did not like being questioned. "Well Duke, let me tell you and any anyone else who wants to know why, and when I am finished I do not ever want to hear about it again." The first reason is this kid here is damn good with his hands. You saw what he did to Jeff and Eddie. He wiped the street with their asses and those two by all accounts are not exactly pussies. Number two, I have looked into his eyes and this boy is calm under pressure. I have seen full grown men who would be begging, crying, and wetting their pants by now but not this one. Number three, I can tell he is homeless and has nowhere to go. He went on to say I had no sense of direction and he could build on that. In addition, he is good with his hands and I can use someone like him. Besides if he does not work out, then we will just do what you wanted to do, but not until then. You tell Jeff and Eddie they were out done by a better man and if they or anyone else touches this boy, I will handle it personally. Now does everybody understand why I offered him a fucking job? Duke responded, "Yes sir, no problem". Tony looked at me, I am right, you are homeless aren't you? Yes sir I am. If you go through that door over there, there is a room about twelve by sixteen feet, clean it out, then straighten up this whole fucking building and you can live in there. You will find a small bathroom back there; he stood pointing down a long hallway. You will be going to work for me tomorrow as my new lot boy. You can wash cars and whatever else I want you to do around here. For now Duke, give him a key to this building, "yes sir," Duke replied. Then Tony walked out. As quickly as he walked out he walked right back in and said, "Hey kid, what the fuck is your name?" I had given this a great deal of thought so, I was prepared to give my new name since I could not go by my birth name, and I replied, "David Cavanaro." Alright Tony replied. He then exited the building. Now I was left with Duke and the other man. Duke told the other man Johnny go to the front office and get David a key to the building. He looked at me and said, "I am going to be watching you very close, if you fuck up I will put a bullet in your fucking head, then I will chop you up, and send you to the land fill. Just try me". With that said he turned and walked out. My first thought was should I stay or not. I could leave that night and no one would look for me, but I decided I would stay. At least I had a place to sleep and clean up.

I started straightening things up and by late that evening I was done. I had a place of my own. It was not much, but it was better than sleeping behind dumpsters.

The next morning at 7:30am Tony came in to the room, saying I was not sure you would even be here this morning. Well, go into the big shop up front and ask for Danny. He is my head shop mechanic. He will tell you what to do and by the way, you get one hundred dollars a week cash and a place to sleep for now. I thought to myself, not bad. Besides I still had well over twelve thousand dollars stashed away. I went up front, found Danny and told him Tony sent me. He said, I have had been expecting you. Grab a broom start sweeping up. Later I will have some cars for you to wash. That is how it went month after month. Sweeping, washing cars, and going to get lunch for Tony, Danny, Duke, or anybody else who wanted me to run some sort of errands.

CHAPTER FOUR

It was December 14th 1964 and I was stepping out for awhile. There was a young lady a few blocks down the street whose company I enjoyed from time to time. On my way back from a visit with her I was walking down the alley behind the car lot when I noticed Tony's office light was on. This was not normal, at least not this late anyway. It was 11:30pm. I started to walk by and blow it off as it none of my business, but I was curious so I walked up to the window and peaked in. I could barely see, but what I saw was Tony taped to a chair. He was being held by two men while another man yelled at him. My first reaction was to go to a phone and call Duke. Just then I heard the muffled scream of Tony. I looked again and it appeared to me as if they had just cut off one of his fingers. Shit, I did not have time to call Duke, so I walked around the front. It was then I spotted the car, it was still running and there was a man inside. After working my way through the car lot I was able to sneak up on him. His window was down and he was smoking a cigarette. I stuck my pistol to his head and told him, "Do not fucking move, give me your gun." He handed me a 9 millimeter pistol with a silencer on it. I told him, "Put your face on the steering wheel and your hands on the dash board." I took the pistol he had just given me and shot him in the head. He was slumped over the steering wheel so I leaned in and shot him in the head a second time, for good measure. I then proceeded to walk to the front door of the car dealership. It was slightly ajar. Just as I approached Tony's office I heard him scream again. That would be his second finger being cut off. Standing at the door to Tony's office I took a deep breath with and with a stud nose .38 in my left hand and a nine millimeter in my right I went into Tony's office. The two men holding Tony down saw me at once along with Tony, the other man had his back to me. Without saying a word I raised my right arm and shot the man with the nine millimeter, the other man to my left was shot with the .38 caliber I was holding in my left hand. The third man turned, but he did not stand a chance. I told him, "If you so much as breathe your fucking dead! Put your gun on Tony's desk and lay flat on the floor with your arms out." He obeyed, and then I shot the other two pricks in the head with the nine millimeter, twice to make sure.

I pulled the tape off of Tony's mouth and cut the tape off of his one arm that was taped to the chair, he finished getting himself out. Tony wrapped his hand up with his shirt since he was bleeding profusely. "Give me your gun," he yelled! I handed him the nine millimeter. Call Duke and tell him to get his ass over here. Have him bring Jeff, Eddie and Johnny and make it fast. Twenty or so minutes had gone by the time they showed up. "What the fuck happened here?" Duke barked out. "David saved my life, that's what happened." Clean this mess up and go get Doctor Adams. Have him meet me at your place. Also, take this piece of shit to the warehouse on 23rd Street and hold him until I get there. David, you're coming with me. We jumped into Dukes car. Tony rode up front while I rode in the back. We went to Dukes place, it was a bar. We both went in the back way towards Duke's office. Doctor Adams showed up just a few minutes later. He has done work for this group of men before. He asked very little and they paid cash. They paid him more than enough for him to mind his own business. He told Tony, "I would like to put you to sleep to fix this hand of yours." Tony replied, "Not a fucking chance. I have business to tend to. You just fix my hand." With that Doctor Adams went to work. Tony lost the tip of his index and middle finger on his left hand. Luckily he was born right handed. After the doctor was done he gave Tony some pain pills and told him what to do and to call if he had any problems.

The three of us went to the warehouse on 23rd street. In a room in the back there was the one man I did NOT kill. His name was Carlos Sattanalia. They all knew of him. He and "Big Tony" were dealing heroin together. Tony had the connections and Carlos moved the product. Carlos had become greedy and he wanted Tony's connections. He would have gotten them if it were not for me. Carlos was bound and gagged to a beam. Tony started cutting off his fingers one at a time. To control the bleeding he would cauterize them with a blow torch. Carlos would pass out from the pain and then they would wake him up to continue. They would continue this dance until all of his fingers and toes were gone. Tony walked up to this bloody excuse for a human being and shoved a steel rod, small in diameter, into his ear. He hit it with a hammer until it came out the other side. Tony looked at the Duke said, "Dispose of this pile of shit." Tony looked at Eddie, (The one I knocked out that day on Cherry St.) and said "Take David somewhere where he will be safe. If anything happens to him you are a fucking dead man!" "Yes sir," Eddie replied. Take him to the lake house and make sure nothing happens. You understand me, Tony said forcefully. "Yes sir," I got it Tony. You can count on me, replied Eddie.

Eddie and I gathered up some of our belongings. There was plenty of cash for us, Tony saw to that. We headed to the lake house. It was a house in a rural part of Minnesota that sat on a several thousand acre lake. This was a place Tony used to get away from time to time a good place to hide. We left Chicago early the next day, it was December 15th. After we drove a couple hundred miles we pulled over and found ourselves a motel. We had not talked much up to this time. We had our own rooms and pretty much went to sleep until the next day. At 6:30am Eddie called my room and told me to be ready to go by 7:30am. He wanted to get there before it was dark. I showered, pack my stuff, and at 7:30am we were back on the road. The conversation was much better that day. We were rested and had time to soak up what had happened. Eddie said that he was to call Duke once a week to check in. Neither one of us knew how long we would be gone or how things would work out. The only thing we did know was that there would be a conflict between Tony's family and Carlos's family. Carlos was a member of the Giania family. We knew that there was no way Carlos did this without permission from Albert Giania himself. Tony would seek revenge. This much we knew. About one hour into the drive Eddie pulled over. He did not say a word. He just walked to the back of the car got into the trunk. Eddie came back, started to drive away, and at that time he threw a bag of marijuana in my lap. This along with a pack of rolling papers and told me, "Roll a couple of joints." I told him, "I have never rolled a joint nor have I ever smoked any marijuana."

"He told me," "Well at least try to roll me a joint." Well, I gave it my best try; I managed to roll two joints. He took one lit it up immediately and I watched him for a minute. Then I lit mine up. I inhaled too hard at first and I coughed until I almost threw up. The second puff went down a little better. I managed to finish half my joint by the time Eddie finished his. He then grabbed mine and he finished it off. At this point we were both officially "stoned". Eddie really started talking now.

Eddie told me he wasn't happy about sitting on the side lines while the fight was back in Chicago, but Tony gets what Tony wants. He also told me that back on that day on Cherry St., when I knocked him out that, that no one had ever hit him that hard and he had been in more than his fair share of fights. Eddie followed up by telling me that he wanted to kill me that day, but Tony and Duke BOTH told him that if something happened to me, that Eddie and Jeff were dead no questions asked. When big Tony tells you your dead, you are fucking dead! We talked about the men I had killed. Even talked about what Tony did to Carlos. Eddie said, "I watched you while Tony tortured Carlos to see how you would react to something like that." He said I didn't react, I just watched, with no emotion. I was horrible, it was offensive, and it was downright viscous, but it *was* right. I did not react. It didn't bother me to see a man have his fingers and toes cut off. Eddie told me, "I have seen these types of things before, but never had I seen anything this viscous and it makes me cringe." Eddie had learned a lot about me that night watching me while Tony tortured Carlos. He said he had always wondered why I never seemed overly happy, sad, or angry. My emotions seemed flat to him, no up and no down. He figured that I was one of those rare people who felt nothing for the most part and that made me a very dangerous person. One who could kill one minute and later seem perfectly normal. No signs of stress what so ever. I never thought of it that way but, he was right. Of course I lied and told him, "It was not that it didn't bother me, but I did not want Tony or anybody to think I was weak." Eddie told me, you're full of shit! As far as I am concerned you are "stone cold", we moved on. This time we started talking about women, sports, and anything else we could think of.

When we finally arrived at the lake house it was just before dark that evening. It was a very nice place, a one story, all brick home. It had four bedrooms, two bathrooms, and a great room with a very large fireplace. No one had been there in months. We went to town to get some supplies. While we were out we stopped to eat dinner. By the time we got back to the lake house, unpacked, and took a well deserved shower it was around 10:00pm. Eddie rolled us a couple of joints. This time I was able to finish mine by myself. We then chugged a couple of beers and called it a night.

The next day I woke up at 6:30am well rested. Eddie was still sleeping, so I started a pot of coffee. Even put some bacon in the skillet. It did not take long before the smell of coffee and bacon woke Eddie up. He wanted to know what the fuck I was doing up that early cooking breakfast. He bitched, but got up anyway. I cooked some eggs and he made the toast. After we ate breakfast we smoked some weed and bull shitted for awhile. We passed the time watching television and playing cards. Only two or three times a week we would go into town for supplies or just to get out of the house. Eddie would call Duke once a week just to check in. Several weeks had passed since we left and things back in Chicago were still pretty unstable. Eddie told me that his cousin Jeff had been killed. Jeff was the other guy I fought on Cherry St. He was the one whose nose I broke. Apparently, Jeff was found by a trash man in a dumpster, shot twice in the head. He was frozen solid, in the wrong place at the wrong time they said. He was not the only one in Tony's family who had been killed. Tony has lost three men so far, the Giania family had lost five. The newspapers were saying there had not been this much violence in Chicago since the Capone days.

By now it was early January and we were both getting pretty bored. I decided to go rabbit hunting one day, Eddie told me I was fucked up. To him it did not make sense to go out in the cold to kill a fucking rabbit when there was food in the house. I liked the taste of rabbit and Tony had a pretty good collection of guns in the house. So I picked a twelve gauge pump. It was a good gun for rabbit hunting. It was snowing outside, but it was not too cold. There was no wind and the trees were covered with snow. I dressed warm and had been out about half an hour. Now there were no signs of any rabbits, but it did not matter. For the first time in a long time I was enjoying myself. It reminded me of life back home in the country.

It was even turning out to be a nice day, or so I thought. While making my way back to the house a car drove by. I stepped behind a tree because I did not want to be spotted. I did not want to take any chances since the car had Illinois plates, this peaked my interest immediately. I watched as they drove past the house and out of sight. I heard the car stop followed the sound of car doors closing. It was unmistakable. This could not be good. I started back to the house at a pretty fast pace, but before I could get to Eddie I spotted two men coming through the woods. They would reach the house before me. I had to stay hidden the best that I could while working my way to the house. They came up on the opposite side of the house from me so I could no longer see them. That was bad, but they could not see me so, that was good. I quickened my pace. Then I came upon the other side and worked my way around the back. When I peaked around the corner one of them was standing on a pile of fire wood peering into the window. The other was watching him and he already had his pistol out, neither man saw me. I drew a deep breath then popped out around the corner. They still had not spotted me. I was now about twenty-five feet away from the man who had his gun drawn and his back to me, I shot him in the back of the head. At that distance his head almost disintegrated. The other man fell back off the pile of wood. I put the shot gun to his head and told him "Don't fucking move". By now Eddie had come out to see what was going on. How the fuck did anybody know where we were at? No one, but Tony and Duke even know we are here. I told Eddie "Go get his gun and check him out." Eddie took his gun and rolled him over. When Eddie say the man's face he said, "I'll be dammed. It is Mikey Falcone."

"Hey Mikey, who's the prick lying over there?" Jason McKendree was the other man according to Mikey. It was hard to tell without half a fucking head. Eddie asked him, "How did you find us?" Albert has known about the lake house for a long time, but we did not know exactly where it was. We just knew the general area. We had been here for two days when we spotted you guys in town. We followed you to find the cabin. We decided to wait and come back today to make our move. I guess that was stupid of us. "That was real fucking stupid" I replied. I then pulled the trigger from a distance of about four feet. His head looked worse than the first prick I shot. Eddie went down the road and brought their car back. We put their bodies in the trunk along with as much of their heads as we could scrap up. The snow was coming down pretty good now, so it would cover the rest of the mess outside. We had to get out of there. We packed up and I drove the car with the bodies inside. We were heading back toward Chicago.

Seventy or so miles down the road we pulled over in a little town and left the bodies in a parking lot. After we wiped the car clean we drove for about an hour. We then pulled over and checked into a motel room. I called Duke to let him know what was going on. Duke told us to stay in a different motel everyday and keep on the move. We were supposed to call Duke every couple of days and to stay away from Chicago. He said he would let us know when it was okay to come back. For the next ten days we kept on the move. We were working our way toward, but around Chicago. Finally, Duke said it was alright for us to come home. We worked out a deal with Albert, but be careful. Call me when you get to town.

The next day we made it back to Chicago and gave Duke a call. He told Eddie to meet him on Philmore St. in front of the apartment building that Eddie lived in. It was three blocks from Cherry St., and Tony's car lot. We pulled up to the front of the apartment building and noticed Duke and a couple of the other guys standing out front. Duke greeted me by giving me a hug and the kissing on both cheeks. I was surprised because this was something done out of respect. I was nobody, just a lot boy. Duke told me he was wrong about me that I was more of a stand up guy then any man he has ever met. He told me that he knew what I had done at the lake house and come spring we need to go back up there and clean up whatever is left after the snow melts. I agreed.

Duke looked at me and said, "Let's go check out your new apartment." We went to the third floor of the building, Room 302. When the door opened there was Tony and all the guys who were important. They cheered saying things like, "Hey Davey, you're alright", "You're a stand up guy", and "You're a bad little son of bitch." Several of them gave me their phone numbers and told me to call them if there is anything we can do to make you some money. Then it was Tony's turn. "He told everyone to shut the fuck up, I have something to say". Everyone in this room knows what David did, and without him I would not be here and neither would you Eddie. Eddie raised his glass to me then Tony told everyone that as far as he was concerned I was the son he never had and that everyone in his family would treat me accordingly, that at the age of nineteen I was the youngest *made man* in his family. Everyone raised their glasses and toasted to me. My apartment had three bedrooms, two baths, and was spacious. Tony took me into the master bedroom of the apartment so we could talk. He told me that my days washing cars were over. That he would personally see to it that I started to make some real money and not to worry about the rent since he owned the building. Tony thanked me again for saving his life. I asked him how his hand was doing. He said that he would be okay and not worry about that. "If you do not like the way we furnished your apartment, change anything you want, it is on me." From now you will answer to Duke. He will give you orders understood? I nodded in agreement. We then returned to the party. It went on for hours. We had food, liquor, and they brought in some hookers. I spent two hours with three of them. What a night, I was on top of the world.

The next day Duke came by and woke me up at 8:30am. He told me to get dressed, "We are going shopping. A made man should dress better then you do." When we were leaving Duke handed me ten thousand dollars from Tony, it was some walking around money for me. I told him, "I appreciate everything Tony does for me and that I would be there for Tony if he needed me for anything." Duke told me that the three days before Eddie and I got back to Chicago the apartment you now occupy was taken by Mr. Osborne. I had seen Mr. Osborne around the neighborhood before. He owned the dry cleaning business we used and was a very nice man. Tony and Duke went to see him, they told him he needed him to move to one of the smaller apartments. Tony said that he had plans for the apartment he was currently living in. They asked him, but made sure he knew he didn't have a choice but to move. They told him that if he did not want to move, his other option was that Duke would put a bullet in his head, cut him up, package the parts, and put them into a dozen different dumpsters. His body would end up in the landfill. Tony told him to let Duke know what he wanted to do then he walked out of the room. I am glad nothing happened to Mr. Osborne. Like I said, he seemed like a nice man.

Duke and I talked for awhile at one point I asked him how Tony managed to work things out with Albert Giania. Duke told me the other families in Chicago forced a meeting, things were out of control. Every other day a body was turning up and the local boys were coming down on everybody. Tony and Albert came to an understanding. Albert paid Tony two hundred and fifty thousand dollars for his two missing fingers and assured Tony it was all a misunderstanding. He did tell Carlos to try and find out whose Tony's connections were, but not the way Carlos was used to doing it. Carlos took it upon himself to do what he had to do. Tony took the money and he accepted the apology even though Tony knew that Albert was full of shit. It was good business.

I was put in charge of collecting money along with Eddie. We collected from local business owners in our area. The people we collected from owed Tony because they had borrowed money from him. We also collected money from people who were gambling, dealing drugs, pimps who ran whores', the guys who ran lunch trucks at construction sites, and construction contractors. We even got money from the guy who had a hot dog cart. Everyone paid and if they didn't, we would do whatever it took to keep the money coming in. Break a few bones, maybe burn their cars to the ground, and if that did not work, well then we would tell them where their kids went to school and how pretty their wife was. They all paid eventually. The money was coming in; my share was fifteen hundred dollars a week. By the time I turned twenty years old I had money to burn and I did not pay any rent. No matter where I went people didn't dare have the nerve to charge me for my meal or drinks. It was all ours. Not even the cops would bother us because Tony had most of them on payroll as well. There were other people who would pay us to steal a car, burn a building for the insurance money, or break the leg or arm of someone they were having trouble with. We called that, "Being paid to send a message."

CHAPTER FIVE

June of 1966 Duke wanted me to kill someone for Tony. Not a problem, I had already killed nine men and I was only twenty years old. One more was not going to matter. The job paid two thousand dollars. This would be the first time I would kill for money. My first official "hit". The man's name was John Lunde. He was the co-owner of a piece of real estate that was about to become worth a lot of money. His partner was Police Commissioner, Michael O'Toole. The commissioner stood to make a great deal of money if his partner was out of the picture. I was given the address and apartment number where he lived. I let myself in and I waited for hours. I started to think to myself," I hoped he is alone, if not I will have to kill more than one person tonight". Finally around 12:30am he came home. I heard the door open, he was alone. He came in, turned the light on, and I came up behind him. I told him, "Do not move!" He started to beg for his life when I told him, "I am just here to deliver a message, so calm down Mr. Lunde". He responded by saying, "Okay, just do not hurt me, please." That's when I was sure I had the right man. One shot to the back of the head and one more to make sure. No one heard me because I was sure to use a silencer. I stole his watch, his rings, took his wallet, and then ransacked the house to make it look like a burglary. After I left I threw his jewelry and wallet in a dumpster. Of course I took what money he had first. The police figured he interrupted a burglary and was an unfortunate victim. It was that easy. The police commissioner was happy, Tony was happy, and Duke was happy. Things ran pretty smooth for me

 I was enjoying myself until August 1966. One night Eddie and I were out, we had finished our last collection for the day. So we went to a local gentlemen's club. We had a few drinks and were enjoying ourselves when four men came to our table. Only one of them took a seat. Eddie knew him, his name was Johnny Nino. They called him "Johnny Jingles" because he had a gift for making money. Turns out that the guy driving the car that night at Tony's car lot, the first one I shot, was his cousin. He just wanted to let me know that if he got a chance someday he was going to even the score. "Watch your back boy; you never know when or where, but someday you are going to pay for my cousin's death". Eddie told me not to worry that he had too much to drink. He would not dare fuck with you since he knows Tony would have him killed. I asked Eddie, "What if he makes it look like an accident?" Eddie looked at me and just shrugged. I knew then I would have to take care of "Johnny Jingles" before he took care of me. Eddie left shortly after; he said he had something to take care of. I decided to stay for a while and enjoy the evening and the girls. Later on this fellow I knew came in to the club. He was alright. He was one of Tony's men. His name was Danny Nero. We sat and had a few drinks together. At some point he decided to start slapping the women around in the club. I suppose because of my stepfather hitting my mother something in me snapped. I wanted to kill this prick. I asked him if he was interested in making some money. He could help me make a collection. He said, "Sure why not." I told him to leave and pull his car down the alley. I told him he needed to give me fifteen minutes. I would meet him in the alley that way we didn't leave together. He agreed and left. I waited the fifteen minutes. On the way to his car I picked a newspaper up off of the ground. I opened it and walked up to the driver side. I asked him, "Did you see this?" I held the paper close to him. As he leaned over to see what I was talking about I shot him through the paper in the head. I leaned in and put two more rounds in his head for good measure, then threw the paper on top of him and walked away. I do not like any man who beats on a woman so that he can feel tough. I consider these men to be cowards.

The next day Duke asked me about what happened to Danny. I acted surprised and told him that Danny was at the club last night, but he left before me. He told me that he had something to take care of. I told Tony if I heard anything I will let him know. Of course I never heard a thing.

Things went by pretty normal for awhile. Then May of 1967, I was out celebrating my twenty-first birthday at Duke's place. Everybody was there, even Tony. I went to the restroom and "Johnny Jiggles" followed me in. "Hey kid," he barked. He was drunk and his three thugs were with him. He never went anywhere without them, not even the restroom. "Jiggles" said, "You know we are not finished. Someday it is going to happen." You have to know that, and by the way, you can cry to Tony again if you want but he can't help you. No one can, he then turned around and they all walked out. I never said anything to Tony, but Eddie did. I knew what I had to do and I knew that I would have to do it before Johnny had a chance to follow through. Maybe he would, maybe would not. I knew that I was not waiting to find out, but I could not tell anyone. Johnny was a *made man* from the Giania family and everybody knows you don't kill a *made man* without permission. I knew that Johnny, like all people, was a creature of habit. This I learned from growing up on a farm and hunting animals. Their habits made them predictable and I would hunt him as I would hunt a deer. I would be patient, study his movements, then strike. That's exactly what I did. I followed him from time to time. I soaked up what I heard about him from others. This went on for almost three months. I decided that the right time and place was between 9:30pm and 10:30pm on a Friday night when he was leaving the booking business.

I had to be sure everything was in place. Just in case I had to get of town. I already had one fake I.D. with my newly found name David Cavanaro. I felt it was best to have another back-up I.D. just in case. The guy I went to did work for a lot of the guys in our crew. His name was Tommy Patterson. Tommy was good at his craft. He claimed nobody could tell his fakes from a real I.D. He charged fifteen hundred dollars and a week to get the I.D. ready. This time my name was David Roberts. He was right, you could not tell real from fake. I paid him then suddenly I realized if I had to leave town and use the new I.D. that Tommy knew my new identity. This was a loose end I could not afford. So, unfortunately while he was bent over getting something out of his desk, I put a bullet through the top of his head and one more when he hit the floor. I did not see any point in leaving my money or any money for that matter. I cleaned the place out of any money I could find and let myself out. I had saved or stole, depends on how you look at it, almost eighty thousand dollars. I had the I.D.'s I needed and I had money just in case I had to get out of town.

There was no doubt in my mind that I would have to kill Johnny and his three thugs, but I needed to be sure I had the right weapon. There was a group of bikers on the other end of town. They were always good for whatever you might need. They hung out at a bar called "The Devil's Pit" and if you did not have a reason to be there, then you better not be there. I walked in and asked for Jason. When he came over to where I was sitting I told him I needed a twelve gauge pump with a sawed off barrel. He told me I should come back in two days. Like clockwork in two days I gave him five hundred dollars and he gave me my shotgun. I did not know it then, but would later regret leaving him alive because he would turn out to be a loose end. I had the I.D., the money, and weapon of choice, but something was missing I did not want to be seen by anyone. I needed a disguise.

It was September 1967 at 9:00pm; I placed myself behind a dumpster in a dimly lit alley. Johnny's car was just seventy or eighty feet away. I had a clear view of the door that he would exit from and I would be ready. He was making his collection for the week like always, every Friday night. Like I said, he was a creature of habit. I was crouched behind the dumpster wearing a black shoulder length wig, a fake beard, and a full length drovers coat to conceal the shotgun. Time moves very slow when you are waiting for something like this. 9:35pm rolled around and Johnny, along with his three thugs walked out of the door towards his car. As they approached the car I came out of the alley. One, two, and now all three thugs down. All head shots from fifteen feet away. They saw me come out of the alley, but turned away. I was not taken as a threat. Johnny was frozen in place unable to move. "Turn around," I barked. He turned and I looked him in the eyes and told him, "If you tell someone you're going to kill them then you should kill them". Even then he did not know who I was, that is until I announced myself. The look on his face was priceless, and then I pulled the trigger. Another head shot, this time at only ten feet distance. I grabbed the briefcase full of the weeks take he was carrying then returned back into the alley. I walked one block through the next alley; I turned left and walked one block, turned right to another alley where I had left a duffle bag with a change of clothes. These were concealed behind a loading dock. I quickly changed clothes and put the clothes, hair, beard and the shotgun into the duffle bag. I disposed of the duffle bag in a dumpster. Now I walked two more blocks made a left, with briefcase in hand, and caught a cab. I went back to my apartment and emptied the cash out of the briefcase. I took the briefcase and threw it in a dumpster. I took a cab to Duke's place. I walked in and sat down like nothing happened. It had been one hour and fifteen minutes since I killed those four men and nobody was the wiser. At 11:30pm Eddie came in. He asked if we had heard about "Johnny Jingles". Eddie told us what had happened. Some guy with long hair, a beard and a full length coat killed Johnny and his three thugs. The guy even grabbed the money and disappeared all in just over a minute. We talked about it for awhile then decided Johnny was a prick, fuck him, and that was the end of that. I had just killed my fifteenth man at the age of twenty-one.

Later, when I got to my apartment I counted the money, all one hundred eighty-six thousand two hundred forty-two dollars. I took care of a problem and made a great deal of money in the process. I had right at two hundred and sixty thousand dollars in total now. I put the money under a floor board that I had pried loose just for this purpose. I would sit on the cash for now let things cool down. This was not the time to act stupid.

Things were going okay, nothing out of the ordinary. That is until the first part of January 1968. This was when Tony decided that Eddie and I were going to Los Angeles, California. Tony had people in Los

Angeles for a number of years already. He wanted Eddie and me to move to L.A. to help with the extortion racket. It sounded good to me, after all it was better weather and more money, so why not.

Just a few days later we were on our way. Tony told us to drive to California instead of flying. It did not make sense to me, but I knew not to question Tony. On the morning of our second day, when I came out of the bathroom from taking a shower, I went to open my suitcase and noticed that the zipper was pulled from the left. I had closed it and pulled it from the right. When Eddie showered I looked through the back of the suitcase. All my money was still there. Maybe I was wrong about the zipper, but something didn't feel right to me. That evening, while in the hotel room Eddie said he was going to the vending machine. He asked me if I wanted anything. I told him that I was good, but thanks anyway. Just after he left I decided I wanted a candy bar, so I followed after him. As I started around the corner where the vending machines were I heard Eddie talking. He was on the pay phone. I was not sure at first who he was talking to but it became obvious to me he was talking to Tony or Duke based on what I was hearing. I heard him say, "Yes I found the money, Okay, Okay, I will take care of it tomorrow and then I will head back. I will see you in a few days and for the record, "This is fucked up". "He is like a brother to me, but business is business." I went back to the room just ahead of Eddie. When he walked in I asked, "What took you so long? "He said," I went up to the front desk to get change." I knew then and there that somehow they found out that I was the one who killed "Johnny Jingles" and his three thugs. I would have to kill Eddie before he killed me. I racked my brain trying to figure out how they knew. I thought I covered all the bases. One thing I knew for sure was that I was right about the zipper on my suitcase.

The next day we left around 8:00am supposedly heading for sunny Los Angeles. We talked about what we would do when we got there. Even about where we would be staying. Eddie said the apartment building we were staying in was really nice. He was continuing on like my friend and as if nothing was going on. If I hadn't overheard the phone conversation, I would've never heard the gun shot to the head when he killed me. That's how it's done. It's always somebody you know on the other end.

We were friends until the last possible second. As we were going through South Dakota I noticed Eddie was really studying the area, no doubt looking for a place to pull over. At 10:30am Eddie suggested we pull over to take a piss. I told him, "That's fine I needed to go to." We drove until he found a spot he liked and pulled off the road about a quarter of a mile. I was out of the car almost before he could even stop the car. When he stood up and looked over the car he was starring at my pistol as it was pointed at his head. "What the fuck are you doing? David what the fuck is going on?" I told him to put his hands behind his head and walk around to my side of the car. If you so much as fucking move wrong I will kill you. He said he didn't understand. He wanted to know what he ever did to me. "You are like my brother" he said. "You mean like the brother you were going to kill and leave out here in the middle of nowhere?" I replied. He swore he had no idea what I was talking about. I told him to walk into the woods with his hands behind his head and if he answered my questions truthfully, and only if he answered them truthfully, I would let him live. How did Tony know I killed "Johnny Jingles" and his thugs? Eddie told me that Tony wasn't sure until I found the money you had in your suitcase. I asked him what made him suspect me in the first place. Apparently the Giania family was putting a lot of pressure on everyone about the killings and the missing money. One of them talked to Jason at the Devils' Pit and asked him if he sold any shotguns recently. At first Jason told them no, but when they informed him if he had and was lying he was a dead man. This would be only after watching his wife being raped and tortured to death, as well as his twelve year old daughter. Suddenly he remembered selling the sawed off shotgun to you. This coupled with the fact that "Johnny Jingles" hated you and expressed more than once publicly that if he ever had a chance, he would settle up with you for killing his cousin. Albert Giania was the one who figured it was you. He approached Tony and told him if he did not take care of this matter and get

Albert's money back that he would seek out revenge in his own way. Neither Tony nor Albert's family wanted an all out war. Tony did what he had to do. He said he would handle things himself, that is everything. David, I swear. Eddie claimed he was pulling over to let me go, that he could not kill me. All I had to do was disappear. He would make up something to calm Tony down. I told Eddie turn around and that I loved him like a big brother. However business is business, I shot him through the forehead. Just a single shot. I waited to make sure he was dead. I took all of his I.D.'s and jewelry. That way when they found him it would take time to identify him, *if* they ever did. That would buy me time to get out it of the state, but where was I to go.

CHAPTER SIX

I ended up in Douglas, Wyoming. Mostly it was because they had a Greyhound Bus Station. I needed to park the car somewhere out of the way and leave it. After wiping the car clean I needed to decide where I was going. I looked at the board for a possible destination and picked Cider Falls, Oregon. It sounded nice like it would be out in the middle of nowhere, a rural setting. That's what I needed. Some place quiet and remote, some place to lay low for awhile. I needed time to think about where to go and what to do next, but first I went into a small general store and bought some blue jeans, a flannel shirt, work boots, and a winter jacket because I was definitely out of place the way I was dressed. I put my new clothes on and proceeded to the bus station.

When I arrived at Cider Falls and exited the bus I realized I was right. This was a small town population under two thousand people. The primary source of income came from logging trees or catering to those who came to enjoy the hunting and fishing. I went inside the bus station to ask where there was a good place to stay in town. The woman behind the counter was pleasant, but quite nosey. She wanted to know what I was looking for, as far as a place to stay. She told me that there was motel down the road and there was a nice lodge on the lake, but there is not much to hunt or fish this time of year. She then went on to ask me how long I was planning on staying. I was not particularly prepared for a session of question and answer. I told her I was working on a novel and that I was looking for someplace quiet to work. I would probably be staying for awhile. She suggested the Cider Falls Lodge. It was about ten miles out of town. It's very nice and it should be quiet this time of year, she told me. I told her it sounded perfect and asked if there was a taxi service in town? She laughed, then smiled and said no, but I will be happy to call out to the lodge for you. I am sure someone will pick you up. Forty-five minutes later a truck pulled up out front, it was my ride.

The woman who picked me up was named Sarah. She was wearing work boots, blue jeans, a flannel shirt and a light winter coat. She had no makeup on, her hair was long and black, she had deep brown eyes, and dark skin. She was the most beautiful women I had ever met in my life. She introduced herself as Sarah Cohen. I told her, for having an Irish name you sure do not look Irish. She told me her father was Irish and her mother was full blooded Crow Indian. All I knew was the mix of the two created the most beautiful women I had ever laid my eyes on. She asked how long I was planning to stay. I told her I had no real time frame and that I am a writer looking for someplace quiet to stay.

When we pulled up to the lake it was breathtaking! The lake was just over fifteen hundred acres and the lodge was a three story log cabin that was about six thousand square feet per floor. Inside the main room was a great ceiling. It was thirty or more feet high with a fireplace that you could actually walk-in. The main room was decorated with stuffed animal heads and fish. The outside of the cabin had a covered porch that wrapped around the entire lodge. This was exactly what I needed at this point in my life, peace and quiet with privacy and time to think. It was perfect.

The room I rented was very nice. The lodge served three hot meals daily. At breakfast the first day I was there it was just me and three other men who were traveling through the area on business.

Sarah served me my meal that morning. We chatted; she told me that I was the only guest staying long term. Other than the occasional stray guest that might stay once in a while this is our slow season. We are pretty much dead until spring. For the next several weeks I spent my time chatting with Sarah and her parents. The lodge had an extensive library with a broad selection of material to read. I pretended to be researching for my novel and writing.

Sarah and I became friends as the weeks went by. I respected her and her parents. I never tried to put any moves on her. She was the first women I wanted that I didn't treat like a whore. The weeks turned into months. It was now mid March. One day while I was talking to her father and I mentioned how much I liked the Cider Falls area. He told me that a friend of his was selling three hundred acres of land on the other side of the lake with over a quarter mile of lake front property. I figured I could build a house and maybe settle into a normal life so I bought the land.

I had land, a new car, and even a bank account with some of the money in it in Cider Falls. The rest of the money I put into four other banks thru out the state, all in my newly found name David Roberts. Life was going pretty good. The only thing that was not going great was with a lot of time on my hands I thought about my family. I wondered how they were doing. I had not seen them for more than three years.

I decided to drive to California and call my sister from there, just in case they had a way to trace the phone call. I figured I would be safe this way. I told Sarah that I had business and that I would be gone for three or four days. We exchanged a long kiss and hugged each other before I left. When I got to California I finally got my sister to answer the phone after three tries. She answered, her voice was so familiar. I was sad and but happy at the same time. "Hi sis, it is David." She broke down crying and sobbing. It was hard to understand her. "Finally, where have you been? Are you alright? Mom is worried sick." I asked her, how mom was doing and if she was okay? I am sorry about what I did, but I had to Debbie, I had to. She replied," David, what you did, wrong or not, there were never any charges pressed. They ruled it a justifiable homicide. You can come home now. You should have never ran away and don't forget that the Lidzenbrau's are well connected in this area." I told her that I panicked and I was not going to jail for killing someone who needed to be killed. Then I asked her, "How are the twins and Craig doing?" She told me, "The twins are fine. They are still at home with mom, helping her on the farm, but Craig had been killed in Vietnam in August of 1967. I was sick to my stomach. It was the combination of knowing that if I had stayed home I would not have went to jail, that I would not have had to kill fifteen more people, and that my life would be different somehow. Not to mention my big brother was dead, killed in Vietnam.

We talked for a little while. She had a son while I was gone. He was named David, after me. She wanted to know where I was, where I had been, and when I would be coming home. I told her that the less she knew the better for everyone right now. I also told her to tell mom and the twins I was okay and sorry for what I put everyone through. Maybe someday I would come home, but I was not ready to talk to her about the details. Not now, not yet. I am happy, and I am safe. However I am not ready to come home. Tell her I am sorry, I hung up.

I went back to my hotel room and tried to take in everything that I had learned. I decided that my life was pretty much fucked. That I would never have a normal life and that I just did not care about anything. The next day I went to the local Marine recruiting station and volunteered. In 1968 that was considered stupid. I knew I would go to Vietnam and that is exactly what I wanted. I wanted to kill and kill a lot. I was going to kill until there was no more killing to do or until I was dead. I did not care what happened to me and I was angry about everything. Especially about my brother and Vietnam was a good place to get rid of some aggression.

The Marine recruiter told me where to be and when to be there. I used the name David Cavanaro. He informed me that I had three weeks until I left. This will give me a chance to take care of loose ends before I left. Now how to tell Sarah, It would not be easy. I told her that I had been drafted and that I had to leave in a few weeks. Let's not dwell on it. Let's just enjoy each other. She agreed. I made arrangements with a lawyer about a will and to put money in escrow to pay my property taxes while I was gone. Now it was time to concentrate on Sarah until I left.

We took long walks, cuddled, and kissed, but never more than that.

The night before I left she came into my room late at night, I heard her come in. She said nothing; she just disrobed. She climbed into my bed and we made love for hours. It was without question the best sex I ever had. My entire body was on fire. When we were finished we held each other for sometime then just as she had came into my room, she left not saying a word. We did not speak a word through the entire time we were having sex. Not one word, but then again not one word was needed.

The next morning when I was leaving we held each other in a long embrace. We didn't say much, we just looked into each other's eyes then I turned and walked away.

Three days later I was on a bus in San Diego, California heading for Marine basic training. I stepped off the bus to the sound of a drill instructor yelling as loud as he could right in my face. It was exactly what I heard it would be like. They gave us a nice hair cut, issued us some clothes, feed us, and gave us barracks to live in. The next morning the drill instructor came in just before the sun was up. He was screaming and hollering, telling us things like what pieces of shit we were, how desperate the marines must be getting to take us in, and that we were not even human beings. They said that we were no more than lumps of shit, but with any *luck* they could turn us into highly skilled killing machines. If we did what they said and paid attention that seven out of ten of us would live through Vietnam.

We had exactly five minutes to be dressed and be outside for physical training. The whole time this stupid shit was going on I was laughing inside. Here stood a room full of men in their underwear and t-shirts, with the same hair cut, standing in front of a bed that looked just like all the other beds. We looked like clones. They wanted to strip us of our personal identities and brainwash us to follow whatever order they gave, no matter what, without question. As far as a being a killing machine, I already had a head start, but I am sure they can teach me far more than I already knew. I decided I would play the good obedient little soldier and pretend that they had broken my spirit then reshaped me into the obedient killing machine they wanted me to be.

I thought I was in pretty good shape, I was wrong. These drill instructors would push you to the point you thought you were finished, then they would push some more and you would keep giving. If not, they knew how to take care of a smart ass or someone who was not pulling their weight. One time one of the boys smarted off and our drill instructors walked the man around the back of our barracks and beat his ass. When they came out one instructor simply said, "That's what happens when you try to be an individual in the marines. If you cocksuckers try to stand alone on the battle field you're fucking dead and you might cause the death of a fellow marine." At the same time he guaranteed us that it would not happen. That was the only time anyone fucked with him. I am actually enjoying basic training.

The guy who slept to my right was twenty-one, years old and from Texas. His name was Grant Alexander. Grant was a nice guy and we became friends quick. We watched out for each other. The best part about basic training was shooting your M-16 on the firing range. It became apparent pretty quickly that only a few of us knew how to shoot. The fifty caliber was my favorite gun of choice and I loved that fucking gun as well. That god damn thing would do some serious damage. We also had pistol training, but nothing matched the fifty caliber. I enjoyed the hand to hand combat training as well. They taught us how to use a knife with expert precision. I was enjoying learning how to hold a man while you cut his throat. We learned how to come out on top in a knife fight. That was good stuff.

Basic was here and gone before we knew it and now it was time for future assignments. I volunteered for Vietnam. So did, my pal Grant and we got what we wanted. It was not long before we were on a ship headed for Vietnam. They occupied our time with physical training and meaningless tasks, but still there was left for playing cards, table tennis, reading, and writing letters. I wrote Sarah and told her not to write me back. I was very fond of her yet it could never be. This was only because of the direction my life was headed. No matter how I felt about her it would never work out. Again, please do not write me. It will just make it harder on the both of us. Writing that letter; made me sad, sick to my stomach, and angry all at the same time. I wanted her and I knew she wanted me, but as I had stated it could never be.

CHAPTER SEVEN

It was August of 1968 and we finally arrived in Vietnam. The weather was hot, very humid, and sticky. One could sweat while sitting in the shade. My pal Grant said "Can you believe we volunteered for this shit?" I looked at him smiled and just simply replied, "Yeah." We were stationed at a base camp. They simply called it "Base Camp 413." They should have named it base camp shit hole.

The helicopter ride in was interesting. There were a few shots taken at us. I could hear bullets hitting the helicopter. Everyone was tense and scared, but tried not to show it. Suddenly someone yelled out, "Tony's hit!" I looked over to see that Tony O'Riley was slumped down in his seat. He took a hit to the chest and was now dead. Grant looked at me. He was speechless. I was more preoccupied with watching my second lieutenant throwing up. He became physically ill at the sight of his first dead body. It was not very encouraging for the men to watch the man in charge; second Lieutenant Mike Albers throwing up, repeatedly. After his piss poor pathetic performance I came to realize I did not care for him and absolutely did not respect him. When we landed he tried to pretend it never happened and that he was in control of the situation.

They assigned us a place to sleep, small dugouts in the side of a hill.

In the first few days we did meaningless tasks like digging new latrines and clearing brush to give a larger area of distance from the base camp to the jungle.

At night we would play cards. We would try not to think about where we were, how we might react in battle, and if we would live. On day six, we were sent out on a reconnaissance mission. We left at day break with our Sergeant. Sergeant Jack English, he was one tough son-of-a-bitch. He was on his second tour of duty in Vietnam. We all looked to him for anything we needed, that included our Lieutenant and the group of twelve men going on reconnaissance. Four of which were green, including myself.

The first day we saw nothing. I am not sure how far we went that day. That night we ate our prepackaged meals, K-rations as we called them. We slept in shifts of two hours each, sleeping then pulling look-out duty. The next day we pushed further into the jungle. It was about noon and we came up on the bodies of four American soldiers who had been killed and purposely left where they would be found. Every one of the bodies we found had been mutilated, they were tied to trees in an upright position, their penis's removed, and placed in their mouths. Sergeant English told us the North Vietnamese enjoyed sociological warfare as much as they enjoyed killing us. He cautioned us to be careful and to be as quiet as possible the enemy could be near.

Later that day around 4:00pm, gun fire erupted out of nowhere. It seemed to be coming from everywhere. This was it, we were in deep. Men were screaming and yelling. Sergeant English was trying to hold us together. The second Lieutenant was curled up behind a log. He hadn't even tried to fire his weapon. The battle lasted for a good fifteen minutes. Then as suddenly as it all started, it stopped.

I was looking for my pal Grant. After searching for a bit, I found him shot in the head. Over half of his face was missing. The sergeant was calling out for help. I made my way over to him. He was fatally wounded. The second lieutenant finally crawled out from behind the log that he was hiding under and he made his way over to where the sergeant and I were. A few moments later the sergeant was gone. My second lieutenant wanted to leave immediately. He said we needed to start making our way back. I asked him, "What about the men? Shouldn't we get help to collect their bodies?" He said there's no time for that. I asked, "Well shouldn't we at least collect their dog tags?" He was insistent that we leave at that very moment. In my opinion he was being cowardly and I had about enough of this chicken shit son of a bitch, so I shot him in the chest with a short burst from my M-16. *Fuck him*! Three rounds through his chest. A lot of good men died that day and maybe if our second lieutenant had helped us fight, instead of hiding behind a log, my pal Grant would still be here. Fuck him!

I took the time to collect the dog tags so that they could be turned in. The last dog tag I collected was my pal Grant. I cannot explain to this day exactly what came over me. Anger for not living a normal life on the farm, anger because of what I put my mother through, anger because of my brother's death, anger because of the life I could not have with Sarah, or the anger because of my pal Grant. All I know is that I went to a very dark place, a place no man should go.

I decided that if the North Vietnamese enjoyed sociological warfare as much as they enjoyed killing American's, then I would give them some of what they have been giving us. I worked my way through the battlefield collecting the scalps of the North Vietnamese, as well as their ears.

I then headed north into enemy territory. For two days I saw nothing. Moving very slowly and very cautiously, I stalked my prey. An opportunity presented itself to me on the second day. A group of North Vietnamese soldiers, about twelve to fifteen men came along. They had four men posted around the perimeter of their encampment. I waited until dark to slowly make my way through the brush. One by one I crept up on each of the four men, slitting their throats, removing their scalps and ears, and then retreating into the bush.

A few hours later I could hear the chatter of the North Vietnamese soldiers as they discovered the bodies of their comrades. They would not sleep very well from this night on. I laid back watching the remaining soldiers and finally broke off into a different direction from where they were going.

Once again I waited. From a vantage point on a hill top I sat and waited. Six days had passed and finally there was some movement. It was a small group of men. There were six of them in all. I managed to kill, scalp and remove the ears of two of them that day. During that night I waited by the second soldier I had killed and when his relief showed up to take over, I made short work of him. Once again I retreated. Shortly after that, the others would discover what had happened.

They were on the move again; I followed them for two more days. I stayed close, waiting for the right opportunity. Finally one of them broke away from the others. He was only one hundred feet away from them. While he was doing his business I came up from behind, cut his throat, collected his scalp and ears, and then retreated. A few moments after I had killed him his body was found. I can only imagine the terror they must have felt. He was probably still pumping blood through the gash in his throat.

Once again, I broke away and headed in another direction, leaving them alive to deal with what they had seen. To wonder what their version would be of what had happened.

Things pretty much went the same for weeks on end. I would wait, stalk them, and then kill them sometimes every day. There were a few times I would go for a week or more without a kill.

I was cautious and calculative. I would let them go by if I did not feel right. I was in no hurry. The weeks turned into months. My scalp and ear collection was impressive. I had started sewing the scalps to a piece of mosquito netting that I had acquired. I was making a head dress. When I fitted it to my helmet, it draped down past my waist. I had sixty-seven scalps on it and two bandoleers of ears. One for the left and one for the right, sixty-seven ears each.

I had not shaved in months, only bathing occasionally in a stream. My clothes were worn and tattered. I became bored of killing the same way so I decided to change things a bit. I captured a North Vietnamese soldier I caught off alone. I hit him from behind and tied him up. Then I took him off somewhere safe. When he awoke, he must have been horrified by the sight of a man covered in human scalps, wearing bandoleers of human ears, dirty and unshaven with long hair. While still alive I scalped him, removed his ears, and then slit his eyes to blind him. After that I took him back where he could be found buy his comrades, to tell the tale of his encounter.

I did this several times. It was the fifth or sixth time, I am not sure, but I was preparing to scalp a North Vietnamese soldier when the gag around his mouth slipped. He cried out in English, "Please do not kill me!" Almost perfect English. I was taken aback by the sound of a voice I could recognize. I kept him with me for three days. We talked a great deal. He had been schooled in America and told me that I was the *one*. I did not understand at first. "You are the one, the one they speak of." I had a name in Vietnamese that loosely translated to "Beast of the Jungle." They said that there was a half man half beast in the jungle. He was the spirit of the fallen American soldier's, that the North Vietnamese had tortured, back to seek revenge. That the half man half beast was retribution and death rode on his shoulder. That he could strike anytime, anywhere, and then disappear. That no one was safe from him. He told me that this man had become a legend. The legend had become a myth and that the myth was impossible to stop. That even if I died, the stories would live on from generation to generation.

On day three, I told him that I had spent too much time in one place. That I had to move on, "Though I enjoyed your company I cannot let you go unharmed." I then gagged him and removed his ears. Then I cut the bindings on his hands and told him he was free to leave. He untied his feet, removed the gag wrapped his shirt around his head, thanked me as he went on his way, and I on mine.

I continued to kill, always taking their scalps. Sometimes I would let them live, sometimes not. I stayed on the move, never in one spot two long.

CHAPTER EIGHT

Months had past; I believe that it was March or April of 1969. My head dress was now ordained with the scalps of one hundred and three Vietnamese soldiers. My bandoleers were full of the ears from the soldiers I had killed. One had all right ears and the other with all left ears. My beard was long and full and dark black now. My hair had grown long and was wild and disheveled looking. I am not sure exactly where I was, but I had a general idea of my location.

While on the move I had found myself a vantage point at the top of a hill. It overlooked smaller hills with sporadic clearings on them and valleys in between. To the north there was a great deal of troop movement by the North Vietnamese. I could see them crossing through a clearing. There were too many to take a chance. I spotted a small patrol of American soldiers. They would be wiped out if they continued to go in the direction they were headed. I could not allow this ambush to take place. After making my way down the hill that I had positioned myself on, I put myself between the North Vietnamese and the American soldiers.

The American soldiers were noisy. I heard them coming from a hundred yards away. When they got close, I mean really close, one hundred feet away, I spoke, "Turn back." They dove for cover. I repeated "Turn back."

"Indentify yourself," they replied. I repeated, "Turn back."

"Identify yourself," they again said. I finally indentified myself. They asked me to show myself. That's when I stepped out from behind a tree. All weapons were on me as I approached their position. As I came closer and walked past one of them, the ranking officer, I heard him say "What the fuck is he, and what is he wearing?" That is when I suddenly realized that I was still wearing my head dress of scalps and bandoleers of human ears. It was too late to retreat; I explained to them that if they did not turn back that they were going to run into hundreds and hundreds of North Vietnamese soldiers.

They listened carefully to what I had to say. They also were looking at me with complete disbelief. I was asked, "How long have you been in the bush?" I told them, "I am not sure. What month was it?" They told me it was May 26. I replied, "For about ten months." The lieutenant said, "They must be headed for base camp 413." I had come full circle. I was within a day's walk from where I started ten months earlier.

The officer in charge knew that the North Vietnamese were coming and that we needed to be prepared. We were to take a three hour march to the east for a pickup at a designated landing zone.

I was asked to remove my head dress and bandoleers. They were making the other men nervous. I told him I could not do that. He insisted; he even made it an order. I declined. He threatened me, but I still declined. The sergeant spoke up and said "Perhaps this is not the time or place to deal with this matter. We need to get back to base camp and make preparations for the attack." The lieutenant reluctantly agreed. The other men just stared. The sergeant started to lead the way. I stopped him. "If you follow me, I can get you there faster. I just came from that area." They agreed to follow me and I got them there in just over two hours. We had time to spare. That left time for the lieutenant to grill me on where I had been for the last ten months and again try to get me to remove my trophies. I once again declined and once again the sergeant was the voice of reason. He took the lieutenant to the side and told him this man has been through a lot and without him we would have been dead, along with a lot of, if not all the men at base camp. He needs help, just let him be.

As planned, two choppers touched down just long enough for us to climb on board. The pilot turned, looked at me and said "What the fuck is that?" The sergeant said, "Just get this fucking bird airborne and get our asses back to base camp." When we landed they were apparently waiting for my arrival. They had been informed about the presence of a wild man and the military police were there to greet me. They escorted me to the bases commanding officer. When the commanding officer came in he greeted me. He even asked if there was anything he could get me. Then he thanked me for what I had done. I gave him what information I had and he thanked me again. Not once did he mention anything about the way I looked. I was then told that I was going to be escorted to a helicopter from here. I was being flown to intelligence headquarters where they will debrief me.

Upon arriving at intelligence headquarters I was once again greeted by the military police. They took me to the building and quickly put me in a room where three officers came in to debrief me.

The questions they asked me were basic. They wanted to know who I was, were I had been, what I had been doing, and of course about the scalps and the ears. We talked for hours. They brought me some food and something to drink. Even after I told them the whole story from the day I came to Vietnam, up until that very moment, they did not quite believe me. After the interrogations were over I was taken someplace where I could clean up.

They took me to a shower room where I was the only one in there. They posted guards at the doors, leaving me to clean up. This was the first time I had seen myself in a mirror in ten months. I could not believe what I was seeing. I didn't recognize the person looking back through the mirror; I must have stared at myself for ten minutes. I then undressed and took a shower. That shower must have lasted for almost an hour.

When I came out my clothes were gone. They had been replaced with new, clean clothing. My scalps, as well as my ears, were also gone. After dressing they took me to get a haircut and a shave. Now, when I looked into the mirror I started to recognize the man looking back. My skin was weathered and dark, my lips were dry and cracked, I was thin, and seemed much older than twenty-three. Doctors evaluated me at a local hospital. My weight had gone from 178lbs to 158lbs. I had tape worms and intestinal parasites. Both were treatable and I would gain the weight back shortly. They decided I should stay for a few days to make sure everything was okay. Sleeping in a bed again was a treat. I slept for thirteen hours that night. When I woke up they fed me and gave me some shots. One of which was a vitamin B12.

Later that day they took me to see a group of doctors whose job was to determine if I was crazy. They tried to find out if I was delusional. These little gatherings with the doctors lasted for two weeks every day. Then one day they led me to a meeting room. I was told to be seated, and then they left me alone. A few minutes later a man came in alone. I did not know who he was, but he defiantly was not military. That much I could tell. He introduced himself as Mike Walters. He told me that he was with the CIA and that he wanted to talk to me with my permission. I replied, "Go ahead." He started by telling me that the government has been aware of me and my work for several months. They just did not know exactly who I was. The stories coming out of the jungle about the "Beast of the Jungle" were quite numerous. He told me that the North Vietnamese were rattled over what was going on. He said that those high in command were not bothered, but the foot soldiers were shaken. They had become paranoid and were not sleeping as well. Their moral was suffering.

He told me that he had spoken to the doctors and they had concluded that I was not insane, but I did suffer from anti-social behavior. They said that I had the ability to kill with the same ease as people turning a light switch on and off. I told him I had no feelings of remorse or regret. For that matter, I had no feelings of shame for the things I had done.

They also concluded that my IQ was somewhere near 140. He told me that put me in the top ten percent of people in the world and that the ongoing question was what to do with me. "We could make a case that you are insane then put you in an institution for life or we could lock you up for crimes against humanity or just simply take you out back and put a bullet in your head. Which might be the thing to do and it had been discussed." He then went on to tell me that he would rather I go to work for the CIA. "Doing what?" I asked. He told me, they want you to go back into the jungle to continue your one man "Campaign of Terror". We will give you whatever you ask of us. Whatever you need to continue what you have started. You see, what you have done has stricken fear into the hearts of our enemy. This will not win the war alone, but is another tool we can use against them. It may help to keep them off balance. I asked what would happen if I chose not to go back. "Where are we then?" I asked. He replied that we are at option number three then. With that information I agreed, but only if done my way. I also had a list of demands I told him. I want to be promoted to master sergeant; I want my own quarters, complete with a bathroom, a kitchen, my own television, a radio, and air conditioning. He agreed. I also wanted it to be known on base that I do not answer to the military, that I answer only to you. He again agreed. I also want my head dress and my bandoleers back. He asked me, "Why?" I want these things for effect I told him. He agreed to give my stuff back. I told him to get my quarters ready soon as possible and once I was settled in I wanted two high class whores sent to me. Not those street whores, but two clean high class, high dollar whores.

Within a few days I had my promotion. I had been relocated to a different base. I had my new quarters as promised, with air conditioning, and I had my two high class whores. I definitely needed that. I had been far too long without female companionship.

CHAPTER NINE

As time went by my strength came back. We again talked and decided I would go back out soon. I was taken up river on a P.T. Boat and dropped me off. They would be back in two weeks.

Upon entering the jungle I again felt a rush. The smell, the sound, it was all familiar to me. God help me. I did love this, I really did. My contact with the CIA, Mike Walters, had requested that I not kill anymore than necessary, but instead to intensify the horror. Perhaps my purpose would be better served if I left them alive, scalped, earless, and blind, so that people would see them and hear them. So that they could testify that the "Beast of the Jungle" was real. I agreed to try not to kill anyone for fun, and for effect leaving them alive *was* probably better.

I spent two weeks in the jungle and as planned I met the P.T. Boat as we scheduled. They took me back to base where I was debriefed by Mike Walters once again. He wanted to know how many I had killed and how many I had let live. He told me that he had already heard of on a North Vietnamese soldier who had been found scalped, blinded, and earless. I told him that he should be hearing about two more found that way and one found dead, throat cut, scalped and earless.

I rested for three weeks. Most of my time was spent with whores or preparing for my next outing. On my next trip into the jungle, on the third day, I had an opportunity to take a North Vietnamese officer as my next victim. He was about three hundred feet away from his men, writing a letter. I suppose to a loved one. I crept up on him, hitting him in the back of the head. I drug him off into the brush where I performed my usual ritual then turned him loose. This was like killing a trophy buck while hunting. It was rare for an officer to expose himself. Up until then I had never had the opportunity to take an officer.

The months passed and I went out on several missions. My count was up to one hundred and sixty eight. Out of this number, fifty-two men were left alive to greater emphasize the sociological damage on the enemy.

It was now January, 1970. I had just come back from a well desired trip to Sigan. I spent my time with the ladies as well as soaking up the local traditions and history of the area. Contrary to what you might believe, Vietnam was a beautiful country. Its people had been there for thousands of years. They have outlasted numerous people who had tried to conquer them and I was sure they would out last the Americans in the long run.

Upon my returning to base I was summoned by the base commander. He was a lifer. He would spend his life in the military; he lived, breathed, and ate the Marine core. His name was Colonial John Ricco, a fellow Italian American, but I suspect with whatever he wanted, my heritage would not help me.

I was escorted by the military police to a storage depot. When we arrived we were greeted by Colonial John Ricco. He began to question me about the nature of my mission. I could tell from the start that this was not going to go well. I could only tell him that I was unable to talk about my assignment. That it was classified top secret and I offered to put him in touch with my contact at the CIA. He then expressed to me that he did not like things going on around him on a base that was under his control that he was not fully aware of. He suggested that I start talking, *immediately*. I respectively declined.

This line of questioning went on for an hour or so. The Colonial stood up, told me that if I was unable to provide the information to him then perhaps his associates would have better luck. He then left the room. Now the real interrogations began. There were three of them, all military police. They tied me to a chair. My hands and legs bound. They started out by asking me the same questions as before. Over and over, this lasted for hours. They finally lost their patience and began to get forceful, hoping I would start to cooperate, but I didn't change my answers. I just simply stated that I could not talk about the nature of my missions. They started to get more violent. This kept up for hours. At one point I began to slip in and out of concussion to take my mind off the pain. I would revisit my childhood on the farm, when my dad was still alive. Mentally going to a happy place would help with the pain, not much, but some. They decided to get creative. They began by pulling my finger nails off, still I would tell them nothing. At some point I completely lost consciousness. When I awakened I was in the hospital.

Two days had past. I could not remember telling them anything. The doctors told me that I was found by some local villagers five miles from base. They had found me on the edge of a rice field barely alive. I was informed that I had four fractured ribs, my cheek bone was fractured, my jaw was dislocated and I had a concussion along with some internal bleeding. Six of my fingernails were removed, but with time I would heal.

The next day my CIA contact Mike Walters came to visit. He asked me how I was doing. He wanted to know my side of what had happened. I told him I was fine, but not sure what happened. That all I remembered was I had been struck from behind and did not remember anything other than that. Nothing could be further from the truth. I remembered enough to know who I would make pay for this. However first I would have to heal, to rest, to recover, then to plan a plot to carry out to achieve some payback.

I spent twenty-three days in the hospital. When I returned to my quarters, to my surprise everything was as I had left it. Nothing had been touched. My cape and my ears were right where I had left them. I found this to be very odd. They had plenty of time to break in and search my quarters, but they did not. This bothered me, "Why not?" I kept asking myself, "Why not?" It did not make sense. I decided not to worry about that and concentrate on completely healing, so I rested.

I received another visit from Mike Walters. This time he was not alone. He had two men with him. He told me, "We need to talk." I sat down at the dining hall table, Mike sat across from me. He asked, "Who is David Cavonaro? Why wasn't I told about him?" I did not understand where this was coming from. He repeated, "Who is David Cavonaro and who are you?" I told him I did not understand. He pulled a pistol out and the two men behind me did the same. Mike repeated one last time "Who are you?" He told me the CIA had completed an extensive background check on me and I was not David Cavonaro. He did tell me that though my ID's were almost flawless, there were a few subtle mistakes, and to the well trained eye they would prove to be fakes. However he did say that they were some of the best work the CIA had seen. So he said what he want to know is who I really was. He told me before I answer I need to understand something, and that was that he will know my true identity or he will deliver my corpse to Arlington Cemetery personally.

I decided to tell him most of the story. How my real name is David Campanilia and how I killed my stepfather, how I had met Tony Tortenellia, and that I had enough of the life in Chicago and decided to join the Marine Corps to get away. Now he had to try and sort things out. He informed me that if what I said was true I *might* come out of this alive."

They kept me under guard for four days while they checked out my story. When Mike Walters came back to see me, he said my story checked out completely except for one thing. You forgot to mention the fact that you are a *made man* in the Tortenillia family out of Chicago. "I asked him," Was that important?" He told me, "*Every* aspect of your life is important. That if we are to do business together, you cannot hold back information. What was no big deal to me might be a huge deal to the CIA." If it was up to him alone, he would decide exactly what to do with me. He could eliminate me or he could further my relationship with the CIA. Mike paused then told me, "In two days I will put you on a plane to Langley, Virginia where you will receive training that would make me more useful to the CIA. Even though you will be trained by the CIA, you will never be a member of the CIA. Instead you will be considered an outside contractor, someone who would, for a price, take care of problems for them, by eliminating the problem." I then asked the question, "You mean by taking care of problems, that from time to time, you want me to kill people for the government?" He responded by saying, "Yes. Is that a problem because you seem to be able to kill as easily as most people turn a light switch on and off, and you seem to be very efficient at what you do. So, do we have a deal here or not? "I told him that there was no problem. Killing seems to be my calling in life. He also told me I was to destroy the ears and the cape. I was told I should burn them in the incinerator behind the mess hall. I nodded.

Two days was not much time to take care of the things that I wanted to do before leaving, but maybe I could take care of one or two of the four things that needed my attention. The next evening, after dark, I went looking for the one of the three MP's that was in charge of my beating. I was pretty sure where to find him. He was for the most part a lazy son of a bitch who spent most of his time driving around the base or sitting behind his desk. I crept up on his office building. I could see him sitting at his desk. I waited, knowing he would probably come out to take a ride around the base. I hid behind a concrete retaining wall waiting. Finally, I saw him get up and leave the building. As he started to drive by I walked out from behind the retaining wall, I wanted him to see me. I pretended to be drunk so I was staggering and stumbling. When I was sure he had seen me, I pretended to fall down as if though I had passed out. He stopped the jeep, came over to me and he pushed me on my back with his foot. It was then that I rolled over and pointed a nine millimeter with a silencer at him. I told him, "You and I need to take a ride." He said, "Of course, I was just following orders."

We drove his jeep to the back of the mess hall and found a nice dark place to park. Then I told him it was my turn to ask the questions. "What's your name?" I said. He told me his name was Sergeant Ray Johnson. Well Sergeant Johnson, who sent you to interrogate me? He claimed it was the colonial. Maybe it was, maybe it wasn't. I asked him the names of the other two men who beat on me. He gave them to me without hesitation. I then shot him through the forehead, scalped him, and removed his ears. After that, I put his body into the incinerator behind the mess hall. I buried the body under some garbage. I knew the next day's incineration would take care of him. I took his jeep and drove it to the other side of base and left it. I crept back to my quarters and was cleaned up and sleeping by 3:00am. I knew that the following day at 5:00am I would be on a plane for Langley. This did not leave me much time.

That night, at midnight, I left my quarters and made my way across base to the colonial's house. There was a guard posted at the front of the house. The house was surrounded by a six foot tall block wall, but lucky for me a light was burned out in the back. No doub it had been burnt out for awhile. In usual military fashion, nothing gets done very quickly. Their own paperwork makes them very inefficient by nature.

I easily scaled the wall and let myself into his house through the back door. I took my time moving through the house. It was very dark, but the sound of the colonial snoring was my guiding light. It took me over thirty minutes to make my way from the back door to his bedroom. The bedroom door was unlocked. Very gently, very slowly, I opened the door. I was standing over him with my knife in my right hand. I put my left hand over his mouth with my knife blade at his throat. He froze. The Colonial was in shock. He tried to speak when I asked him, "Do you remember me?" Then in one motion with my right hand I cut his throat so deep that I felt the knife hit the bones in his neck. After he had finished bleeding out I scalped him and carved off his ears. Just as I came in, I left. I then went back to my quarters, cleaned up again and finished packing. It was 4:00am and my ride was picking me up. I would be on a plane for Langley before they even knew that colonial was dead. The other two would have to wait.

CHAPTER TEN

Once on the plane I slept almost all the way to my destination. When I arrived at Langley they gave me a place to sleep and a meal to eat. The next day my training began. My training was one on one. I was not allowed to talk to anyone except my handler. We spent a lot of time learning to use a knife. We spent time everyday on hand to hand combat. I did not know that there were so many ways to kill a man with your bare hands. We spent a great deal of time on pistols, rifles, and especially on long distance shooting. They wanted me to be able to kill a man from over half a mile away. My enemies would be dead before they heard the shot. We also trained extensively with explosives it doesn't take a great deal of C-4 to do a great deal of damage.

A few weeks into my training I received a visit from the man who recruited me, Mike Walters. He took me to a room where we could talk. He seemed agitated. I asked him, "You okay?" I told him that, "It seems to me that something is bothering you." He told me, "You are one crazy son of a bitch. I know it was you who killed the colonial and was no doubt responsible for the disappearance of Sergeant Ray Johnson." However, what I didn't know was that the colonial was operating on the direct orders of the CIA. They had staged the whole interrogation, the beating, everything. They wanted to see if I would talk, if I could be trusted."

"The colonial was just following orders. They all were just following orders," Mike explained. In my mind that explained why no one searched my quarters. Now it all made sense. I was not sure what to tell him other than the fact that it was too bad that I didn't have that information before hand. It might have made a difference. He responded by screaming at me, "You cannot go around killing people, *especially* Americans at your will. God damn-it David, this is not acceptable" He continued; "I should have guessed that something like this would happen when you told me you did not remember anything about who beat you." He told me, you are almost as dangerous to the United States government as you are to our enemies. You had better hope you always remain a valuable commodity to the United States government. And never do anything like that again." After he calmed down, he told me that though he understood what I did he could not allow that kind of run-away rouge behavior from his people. I assured him that, "I will try to make sure that nothing like that happens again." When he left I believed we were on good terms.

My training continued over the course of nine months. I trained six days a week on weapons, explosives, and we also touched base on foreign language. Only enough German, French, and Spanish can get by as a tourist if necessary. Finally, my training was far enough along that I was able to find myself an apartment just outside of city limits. I settled in and I was given contact numbers to call every Sunday at exactly 5:00pm eastern time. Mike Walters said, "Everyone needs a code name, yours is an easy one. You will be known as "The Butcher." He thought that was pretty funny. He even laughed when I called in. The person on the other end would always say, "Speedy Glass. We fix your glass in a flash." Then I would say, "This is the butcher. I am having a meat sale. Are you interested?" We would have a brief conversation, always the same, every Sunday at 5:00pm eastern time.

January 1971 came around along with my first assignment. I was to go to the local airport. My tickets were for reserved coach class. I was headed to Mexico City, Mexico. Upon my arrival I was met by my contact, he gave me a weapon and a cyanide pill. I was supposed to use this only as a last resort. My target was a Mexican business man. Why?

I didn't know nor did I care. It was not my concern. All I knew is that the CIA wanted him to go away and I was being paid twenty-five thousand, tax free, dollars to make it happen. The money was being deposited in a Cayman Island numbered account that I had started at the request of Mike Walters.

The man in question was Jesus Pilla. He was a well to do businessman. He was the owner of a spacious estate just outside of the city. He was driven to town and back every day. Large Rottweiler's guarded his estate in the evenings. He even had a personal body guard whom lived at the estate, along with a housekeeper, his two children, and his wife.

On January 18th, I drove within a mile of the estate. After parking my rental car off the road where it was concealed I made my way to the estate. The first obstacle was the dogs. I had brought with me a pound of raw hamburger which I had mixed with the cyanide capsule the CIA had given me. I then approached the rod iron fence. The dogs came over to where I was barking loudly so; I threw each one of them a portion of the hamburger. They consumed it rather quickly and within moments they were lying on the ground, mouths foaming, dead. I then entered the compound. Once inside I climbed up a trellis that had vines growing on it. I found myself on the second floor balcony just outside of Mr. Pillas bedroom. I was dressed completely in black, standing next to a large potted plant, just a few feet away from the French doors leading to the bedroom of the man I had been hired to murder.

Suddenly, the French doors opened and Mr. and Mrs. Pilla came outside. They walked to the hand rail at the front of the balcony. I knew that if they turned in my direction they would no doubt see me. I took three steps forward and with a nine millimeter, which had a silencer on it, I shot his wife in the back of the head. Before she fell and before he could react I shot him in the back of the head also. After they had fallen to the floor of the balcony I put one more round into each. I then left by the same manner in which I had came.

I stopped on the way to the car to change my clothes. I disposed of the pistol and clothes went back to my place. For the next two days I took in the sights, playing the part of a tourist. On January 20th, I boarded a plane once again, this time for Langley. I had just made some good money. All expenses were paid by the United States government and it was a pleasant break from my boredom back home.

Months had passed when finally another assignment was handed to me. My next mission would take me to Ireland. My target was a man named Patrick O'Brien. It was April 1971, and just as before, I met my contact shortly after arriving in Ireland. We discussed the details of my mission. My target lived in Dublin. He was a wealthy, well connected, man with political aspirations. However he was stirring up problems for the Irish government which in return caused problems for the United States.

I stalked him for six days to get familiar with the area as well as him. On day six I followed him into "Donavan's" a pub that he frequently visited. I was wearing a pair of fake eye glasses, fake beard, and had a mole placed on the right side of my face just above the fake mustache. I sat down and ordered a pint and then I waited. When he stood up and walked to the restroom, I followed him in. When I walked into the restroom I noticed that no one else was in there. I walked up behind him and with my right hand I placed my palm on his left cheek, then placed my left hand on the back of his head and proceeded to snap his neck. I quickly placed him in the restroom stall, pulled his pants down; and locked the door. I slid out from underneath the stall then went back to my seat to finish my pint. I then thanked the bartender, and excused myself. I walked a few blocks, and then ducked into an alley to remove my disguise along with my jacket. I tossed them into a dumpster and when I came out of the other end of the alley I was a different person. I went about my business as a tourist. A few days later I was on my way home.

After I arrived back home I spent some time at the CIA training facility in Langley. I was to learn the art of changing my appearance with the right hair piece or facial hair, or a well placed mole, a fake scar, glasses, a hat, or sometimes even a fat suit to put on twenty or thirty pounds. I could appear to be someone else whenever I needed to be or *wanted* to be. I furthered my language skills and practiced more at the shooting range. It was an easy and entertaining way to occupy my time between assignments.

CHERRY STREET: MADE TO KILL

In July 1971, I was called on again to do a job in Frankfort, Germany. The gentlemen's name was Otto Schillinger. I am not sure why he had been targeted for removal, but it was of no consequence to me. All I knew was that this job paid forty thousand dollars, plus expenses. Mr. Schillinger lived a few miles outside of town in a beautiful villa. The home must have been at least a hundred years old. It had been updated, complete with a swimming pool. The villa had no roads leading to the rear, only the main road and a private road. The private road was three quarter of a mile long. No good. After a few days of studying the layout of the land, I decided to hike in. His property backed up to some government property which allowed back packing and camping. I took a couple of days to get my gear together and I was off.

I was perfect American tourist who enjoyed back packing and camping. I was able to place myself within three miles of his villa when I made camp. I left out before the sun went down. I was within eye sight of the villa just before sunset. I took the time to lighten my load and take just the things I required. I changed my clothes so now I was in all black. I even blackened my face with makeup. With my pistol in my hand I headed for the villa. When I arrived in the backyard of the villa I placed myself behind a row of well grown bushes. I watched and I waited. After just a few minutes Mr. Schillinger, his wife, and two children came from around the side of the house. They were going to go swimming right in front of me. I was less than fifty feet from the entire family as they enjoyed themselves on this warm summer evening. They swam and they played for several hours.

Finally, close to midnight, his wife took the children in to put them to bed. This was my opportunity. As the children went into the house Mr. Schillinger lit a cigar, leaned back in his chair, and relaxed. I slowly crept up on him, gently placing my pistol to his head. Without making the slightest of moves he told me that he had been expecting me or someone like me for quite some time now.

He asked that I please not harm his family. It was then that I decided to give him my cyanide capsule. I told him that if he did as I told him his family would remain unharmed. I then told him to put the capsule into his mouth and bite down. It would be quick and relatively painless. This would be for the best, to be found this way instead of being found with a bullet in your head. He took the pill, held it in his hand, and then he thanked me. He then placed it in his mouth and bit down. He convulsed for a moment then relaxed. Just like that Mr. Schillinger was dead. Other than the small amount of discharge coming out of his mouth, he looked rather pleasant. He knew this day was coming. He expected it, he took it with style, and died with grace. He was one of the few men in my life that I would kill, but yet on some level admire at the same time.

    I retreated to my campsite where I rested until early that afternoon. It *was* truly a beautiful country. The people were pleasant and the food was tasty. I stayed for another two weeks and just relaxed and took in the sights.

    After arriving home I spent some time with a lady friend. I had made her believe that I was working for the government. That my job was writing research papers and that my work quite often took me to other parts of the world. I would never know for sure were and how long I would be gone, she accepted that. She was always glad to see me and I enjoyed her companionship.

CHAPTER ELEVEN

In early August I received my next mission. This time it was two lawyers, both of whom were located in Paris, France. As always the cover was an American on vacation under an assumed name. Upon arriving in Paris I meet with my contact to receive further information about the task at hand.

The next day I went to the building where the father and son had their law practice, Ladue and Ladue Attorneys at Law. It was an eight story building in the older, but well kept part of the city. I studied the lay-out of the building. I spent two days trying to figure out how to get both men in the right place at the right time, so as to make the hit work. I knew that if one or the other where to be killed the remaining one would probably disappear. I thought I could just wait to get both of them in any one place at one time and walk up with guns blazing, but that would not only be messy but also unprofessional. Not to mention the strong possibility of getting caught. I had considered placing explosives in their offices, but it would have to be in sufficient quantities to cause the complete destruction of their entire office complex to make sure, depending on their exact location in the office, I would be able to ensure that they were both killed. This would also be messy. The people who occupied the office space on either side of them would no doubt suffer deaths and severe property damage. Not to mention the problems associated with the falling debris plummeting to the street below on the innocent bystander. So, that plan would not work either.

They came to work separately, even lived in different areas. The buildings they lived in had good security. They showed up at different times on any given day at their office. *Finally*, I had the solution to the problem that I had been trying to solve. I knew how I was going to make two hits within moments of each other. The answer was in the building across the street. It was an apartment building and apartment #310 was located directly across from the attorneys' office. It would give me a direct look into their offices. I could see into the father's office as well as into the sons from this single location. All I had to do was gain access to the apartment in question and then be patient.

I discovered that the apartment room I wanted, #310, was currently being leased by a retired school teacher. I had my contact dig into his life's history. He was a 68 year old widower who had no children, and rarely left his apartment. He was a bit reclusive. I decided to set off the fire alarm in the apartment building. When he exited the building, while in the cover of the crowd, I gave him a quick shot with a hypodermic needle. The cocktail inside put him into immediate cardiac arrest. He was dead in moments.

The next day I went to see the building management to inquire about any rooms for rent. I insisted on a view of the street and preferred a room not to high up in the building. The building management told me that the gentlemen in apartment #310 had died of a heart attack just yesterday. He told me that they were in the process of gathering up his personal belongings to put into storage since he had no relatives to speak of. The furnishings came with the lease. There was just one problem though; they had a long list of people who had signed up for an apartment. So when one became available they would go down the list from the top, otherwise it would not be fair. I was told they would be glad to add my name to the list. I reached into my pocket and slid five hundred dollars across the desk and asked if that would help. The gentlemen told me, "That would not be proper." I then slid another five hundred dollars across the desk. He then decided that he must have overlooked my name on the list. "There it is on the top of my list," he replied. It would be a few more days before I could take occupancy of the apartment.

Finally, I had the room I needed. It was perfect. I sat up a high powered rifle with a scope and a silencer in the living room. Now all I needed to do was wait, wait for the exact moment that they were both in their offices at the same time. I needed at least one of them to be seated.

I installed curtains in the living room. They were beige in color and somewhat resembled mosquito netting. It allowed someone to see through them, but it made it difficult for anybody else to see in. That would not be a good thing if someone could see into my living room where I had a high powered rifle mounted on a tripod. I am quite sure that it would not work to my advantage.

The first day I would see one or the other in their office at different times of the day but never at the same time. I stood watch, looking into their offices from my living room, from 8:00am until 6:00pm. This was repeated for the next few days, reminding myself that if I waited long enough and stayed patient that my plan would pay off. To occupy my time during the day I moved the television set so that I could watch it as well as keep a constant watch on their offices. I had a cooler with drinks and food, even a container to urinate in so that I did not have to leave the living room from the hours of 8:00am and 6:00pm. I knew that when I finally got them in the exact place at the same exact time that my window of opportunity would be small. I could not afford to be going to the bathroom, getting something to eat, or drink at a crucial moment that might not present itself again for quite some time.

Finally, the week came to an end. Three days of waiting and watching to no avail. It was Friday night and I had been in the apartment for three days without a break. I needed to get out. I needed to go someplace where I could take off the gloves that I wore constantly. Always careful not to leave finger prints. I was always careful to cover my tracks. I decided I was going to get out for awhile. I put on my disguise. The same disguise that I wore when leasing the apartment. I wore a mustache with a mole placed on my right cheek, a pair of clear non prescription glasses, and a ball cap. This was a familiar disguise that I used from time to time and it was easy enough to get into and out of.

I went outside where I was met by a taxicab. I told the driver to take me where a guy can find some action; you know to have a good time. He took me to Layette Street. The street ran on for miles. It was lined with clubs, restaurants, and an occasional hooker. I went from place to place, had a drink and moved on. The fourth place I went into would turn out to be the start of yet another adventure.

When I walked in I immediately saw one of the two remaining marines who was involved in interrogating me back in Vietnam. Out of instinct I immediately recoiled. After a few moments it dawned on me that I was somebody else and they would never recognize me. It was then that I felt like Christmas had come early and Santa Claus had delivered me a special present. One particular marine in the bar was the one who pulled my finger nails out. He was a large man, six foot four inches tall, two hundred thirty to two hundred forty pounds, fiery red hair, and was in his late twenties. I still remembered his name. Joseph Flanagan. A fine Irish name for a "Fine Irish Prick."

I walked up to the bar and in broken French I ordered a vodka and tonic. I sat right next to him not speaking at first. I wanted to make sure he did not recognize me. After a few minutes he tried to order another drink, but the bartender did not pay him much attention. I asked him, "Can I help?" I told him, "I speak some French. Not much, but enough to get by." He told me he would appreciate that. So I ordered him a Jack and Coke. He tried to give me some money I told him not to worry about it; I would take care of it if he did not mind. I told him I was just glad to have an American to talk to. He thanked me for the drink and the help.

So there we sat for all intensives purposes, me and a dead man. As far as I was could tell he was totally unaware that his life was going to be cut short. We drank for hours, talked about sports, and where we were from. I told him that I had been in town for three weeks and that

I had an apartment. That I was here because my family owned a import-export business and that we were opening a office in Paris to export French goods to the United States and to import products to France from the United States. Even though it was not particularly what *I* wanted to do for a living. After getting out of the military I had to make a living somehow. He was not dressed in his military uniform, but I knew this conversation would bring us closer together because we shared the same background. He responded just as I knew he would. He asked me, "What branch of the military were you in?" I replied, "The Marines and after Vietnam I did some time state side before I got out." It was then that he informed me that he was in the Marines and that he was here on leave. He decided that Paris would be a long welcomed break. He said that he was currently stationed in Germany, but he had also spent time in Vietnam. We talked about our common experiences while in Vietnam and serving in the Marine Core.

It was getting late now. I asked him where he was staying, and no surprise he told me. I offered to pick him up the next day around noon. I told him that I had planned to visit some of the wineries to consider exporting their products and take in some of the French countryside. If he wanted to ride along, we could drink some wine and maybe later come back to town, to the red light district and pick up some whores. We could take them back to my apartment. He agreed, "It sounds like a plan." I told him, "I will pick you up around noon".

Early the next morning I rented a car and drove myself to a café. I had a late breakfast and as promised at around noon I picked him up at his hotel. We drove about one hour out of town, we took a tour of a winery, tasted the different wines, had some cheese, and crackers. I was enjoying myself and as was he. We took two bottles of wine with us for the evening.

The day was still early. The French countryside was breathtaking as I was driving. Finally I was getting used to being on the left side of the road. I spotted a place to pull off the road. I suggested that we pull over and take a walk down the hill to an out crop of boulders, overlooking the winery that we had just left to drink our wine, relax, talk about whatever, and then head back to Paris to get something to eat. After that, we would go fine some whores, he liked this. As he seemed to always put it, "Sounds like a plan."

We had finished the first bottle and started on the second. I stood up and I told him I needed to relieve myself. I walked away for a minute because I actually did have to relieve myself, but before I came back I retrieved the knife that I had taped to my leg. I brought it from my apartment the night before. I sharpened it then I fashioned a sheath out of cardboard and then tape it to my leg just above my shoe.

His back was turned to me as I approached. I started to second guess myself since he had turned out to be a pretty decent guy, but that only lasted for a moment. He was sitting on a rock, back turned, his head back, eyes closed as if he was taking in a deep breathe through his nostrils, and just soaking in the countryside. At that moment I took my right hand and placed the blade of my knife to the left side of his throat while putting my left hand on top of his head. I grasped his fire red hair in my hand all at the same time. This was a familiar scenario to me. He was definitely startled. "What the fuck are you doing?" he asked. I told him, "If you are going to pull out a man's fingernails, beat him, and then leave him for dead, you might want to make sure he is really dead." It was then and only then that he realized who I was. He told me he was just following orders. I told him unfortunately those orders will cost you your life. I then cut his throat hard and deep, to the bone. I let him stumble around for a moment until he bled out. It didn't take long, but then again, it never did. After he was dead I removed his scalp and ears. Some old habits are hard to break. I hid the body where hopefully it would not be found right away.

I went back to Paris. I dropped off the car and went back to apartment. I ate some dinner, and then took a well deserved night's sleep. I woke around 9:30am the next morning and spent most of the day just lying around. I rehearsed what I had to do regarding the lawyers and how to exit the country in a timely fashion. The next morning would be my big day. I woke up early, showered, and dressed. I prepared my cooler with enough food and drinks for the day, I made sure I had a container to urinate into, and I changed my appearance to match my phony passport. This meant adding some grey to my hair and putting on my gray beard and mustache. I wiped down any prints I may have left before I put my gloves on. The same routine, but today would turn out to be my lucky day.

At 10:45am the father entered his office. A few moments later a client entered his office. Eleven minutes later the son walks into his office. He stood at the window just peering out of it. I took the son first a flawless shot to the heart. The father looked to his right. He must have heard the window break as the bullet passed through it he leaned forward as if though. He was getting ready to stand when my second shot hit him right thru the base of his neck. The male client he had reacted by running out of the room.

I stood up, grabbed the one suitcase I had packed, and I simply walked out of the apartment and down the steps. I then walked two blocks and stopped at a café. I ordered myself a coffee and asked the waiter to get me a cab. While waiting for my cab several police cars and an ambulance came by. I paid my bill, took a cab to the airport, and caught the first available flight home to Langley. It was as if I was never gone.

Some weeks later Mike Walters and I had a meeting at a public restaurant. He said, "The work you have done in France was quickly making you the man of choice when needing to eliminate a problem." He also mentioned that the body of a United States Marine was found outside of Paris in wine country. He was found scalped, ears removed, and his throat slashed. He told me, "There is only one man left and I do not suppose you are going to let this go, at least until your finished. Are you?" I sat there in silence, not speaking showing no change in my emotions. Mike then asked me, "Where does that leave us?" I told him, "I do not understand the question."He replied by telling me," If you have to get even with everyone involved, what about me? I gave the order; that it had all started with me." I told Mike that I understood why he gave the order. I know he had to know if I would break under pressure and that I could be trusted. It was vital that Mike knew this one way or the other, but as far as the men he used to carry out his orders, well they must pay. I will not let this go until the last one has been dealt with. I reassured him that I would never harm him. I gave him my word on this matter. I told him, "If you come to me at any time in your life and asked me to perform a hit for you for your own personal reasons that I would take care of it. No questions asked, and I would never mention it again. I now consider this subject closed." He told me he believed me and we shook hands and parted to go our separate ways.

CHAPTER TWELVE

I had been home a few weeks now and I was in need of some companionship. I decided to give my friend Brenda Morrison a call. She was pleasant and didn't ask much of me. She didn't pry into my life, she just let me be and allow me to visit from time to time. I tried to call, but she did not answer so I decided to drive to her house. When I arrived I knocked on her door there was no answer, but her car was in the driveway. As I was walking back to my car her neighbor lady approached me. She asked, "Can I help you?" I told her, "Brenda is a friend of mine and just dropped by to see her." It was then that she informed me of Brenda's whereabouts.

She was in the hospital. I asked, "For what?" The neighbor lady told me, "Someone broke into her house and had beaten her very badly just two nights ago." After finding out what hospital she was in I immediately went to see her. When I entered her room I was not prepared for what I saw. She cried when she saw me. We talked. I asked her, "Do you know who did this to you?" She shook her head no. I could tell she was holding back. "Brenda tell me the truth!" She broke down crying then told me that she had been raped then beaten by her ex-husband. I asked her if she told the police. She said she had not and then she proceeded to tell me that her ex-husband told her yesterday when he came to see her, that he was sorry, but if she told anyone when he got out of jail he would kill her.

He was an evil man that was considered a bad ass by many people who knew him. He had beaten her before and even had his way with her, but never like this. I could tell she was scared and did not know what to do. I told her that she shouldn't live this way and that she should never tell anyone else what you just told me. I reminded her that if she gave me his name, I knew people who could make this scumbag go away forever. That is if she wanted, or she could live the rest of her life wondering when he would strike again. He would never stop until she was dead. She asked me, "How much?" I told her, "There are people who owe me, so do not worry about how much. Just let me take care of this for you and no matter what, we will never discuss this subject again after today." She paused for a moment then said, "Allen Morrison." She then gave me his address. I asked, "Are you sure?" She nodded. I told her to rest. I would come to see her in a few days.

Later that night I went to his apartment. I rang the bell, Allen answered the door. I stuck a pistol to his head and walked him back into the apartment. He began to speak, but I told him, "Be quiet. Are you alone?" He said, "Yes." I then barked at him; *"Get down on your knees!"* He began to beg. I walked around him and from behind I hit him in the head with a black jack. If you are not familiar with a black jack, it is two pieces of leather sown together with a piece of lead in it. I have found it to be a very effective tool. The impact of the black jack rendered him unconscious. I remove all of his clothes and placed him on the kitchen table. He laid face down legs dangling over the edge. His feet almost touched the floor. I took the rope that I had brought with me and tied it around his ankles under, the table, and to his wrist. I repeated this on the other side to keep him in that position. I placed a gag in his mouth, so he could not cry out. I sat in front of him drinking a bottle of beer that I had gotten out of his refrigerator. I drank half the bottle then I poured the rest over his head, letting it run down his face. He started to come around. Now it seems as if Mr. Bad ass was not so bad after all. He was on the other end of what he had done to my friend Brenda.

When he was completely awake I reached around from behind, grabbed his testicles with my left hand wearing a glove of course, and in one motion castrated him. He screamed out in pain, but no one could hear him. I then showed him his testicles still in there sack. He would rape no more I told him. I then took the empty beer bottle, poured liquid soap over the neck of it and inserted it into his ass, took a step back and kicked it with my right foot, sending the entire bottle into his rectum, only the end of the bottle was left to be seen. His rectum was split open, blood poured from both his rectum as well as from where I had castrated him. Now he has experienced a rape. I hope he enjoyed it.

By now he had passed out from the pain and loss of blood. I revived him by pouring a pitcher of water over his head. I took my left hand, held his head up and told him Brenda said, "Hi." I tilted my head to the right, then to the left, and finally I cut his throat. He was finished. Before leaving I removed his penis, putting it on his back along with his testicles. Like I said, I never have cared for men who abuse women.

The next morning I went to visit Brenda; she had passed away the previous night from her extensive internal injuries. I was saddened by her loss; not because I had loved her, but because she was a friend of mine. At least her ex-husband paid for what he had done and that I did take pleasure in. I decided that I needed a break.

I called into my contact on the usual day and the usual time with the same cloak and dagger conversation we always had. I informed him, "I will be unavailable for contact for a period of four weeks. I am taking time for myself." I then hung up the payphone I was using, got back into the cab, and headed for the airport. There I caught a flight under the name of Mr. Roberts.

Some hours later I was in California. I rested that evening in a hotel. The next day I rented a car and was on my way to Cider Falls, Oregon to see Sarah. On the long drive I wondered if she still felt the same. How she looked or even if she cared to talk to me anymore. It had been three and a half years since I saw her or spoke to her. I hoped she was still not spoken for, but I knew that she had probably moved on. At any rate I still wanted to see her and take time for myself.

When I pulled up to the lodge, it was just as I had left it. I put the car in park and started the short walk that led up the stairs to the front door. The walk seemed to last a long time. My mind was racing. When I walked in, I did not recognize the man at the desk. I asked, "Do you have any available rooms?" He said, "We do. How long will you be staying?" I told him I would be there for a few weeks. As he handed me my keys to the room I caught my first glimpse of Sarah. She was waiting on a customer in the dining room. I stood and starred for what seemed like long time. I know it was only a few moments, but in those few moments I was looking at what appeared to be an angel. She was *perfect*! The way the sun was coming in around her made her appear to glow. Then she spotted me. The look she gave me was one of discomfort. She quickly exited the room. I felt like my worst fears had been realized; that she wanted nothing to do with me.

I started to leave, but instead I stopped and went to my room, hoping that she was only shocked by my presence. After all, she had no warning. I was in my room for less than fifteen minutes when there was a knock at the door. My heart raced. I opened the door to see Sarah standing before me. Crying, "Why didn't you write me to at least let me know you were alive? I thought you were dead you bastard!" She became mad, "You thoughtless son of a bitch!" I tried to calm her down by saying, "I am sorry." Sarah said, "I have to go now. I do not hate you, I'm just glad that you are okay. We will talk more later on. Oh, by the way the man who checked you in was my husband," then she left the room.

In just a few minutes my emotions went from joy and excitement to sudden depression. The thought of her with another man devastated me. This was too much too fast. When I came down for dinner she waited on me. We spoke very little, after all she was now a married woman. While pouring me a glass of tea she decided to tell me, I have a child, a boy that is three years old. His name is Michael. She said, I named him after your middle name. After hearing this I hardly slept that night.

The next morning at breakfast, another women, waited on me while Sarah worked another part of the dining room. After breakfast I went outside on the large porch that surrounded the lodge and had another cup of coffee. By this time most of the guests had left the lodge to go fishing or hiking. Deer season was not in yet, but would be here in a few weeks. As I finished my coffee Sarah came outside to see me. She told me, "Your letter had crushed me and soon after that I started to date my husband. I soon realized I was pregnant. It was then that we married." My parents decided to bring him into the family business. He works the desk sometimes, but mostly guides fishermen and hunting expeditions. His name is Daniel Sutton. Sarah Sutton, I definitely did not like the way that sounded.

She made no apology for having married, but then no apology was expected. After all, it was I who left her. We chatted for a few more minutes and out of nowhere her mother rounded the corner carrying Sarah's son, Michael. He was a handsome child. He had her dark skin, her dark hair, and brown eyes. When her mother put him down he ran to Sarah. She scooped him up and gave him a big hug. Sarah's mother immediately came up to me and told me that she was glad to see I came home safe. I pretended to talk to her, I pretended to care what she said, but I could not take my eyes off Sarah and her son Michael. By her naming him Michael after my middle name, I felt as if though we were still connected.

Shortly after that her father came outside. When he did Sarah, her son, and her mother went inside. Her father and I talked for hours. He decided that the next day he would take me fishing since I had not been fishing in years. It seemed like a good idea.

Early the next morning he knocked on my door. I got up and went downstairs to meet him. The kitchen was already open to accommodate the early morning hunters and fishermen. Sarah waited on us. I couldn't help the way I felt when I saw her. When she poured my coffee she leaned over my right shoulder. She smelled heavenly. I took a deep breath trying to soak up the aroma and when she turned to leave I looked back to her father. He looked at me as if it was one of those awkward moments in life.

Later that morning we were fishing we were catching some fish and we were enjoying ourselves. When he said, "You know Sarah's a married woman now, whether I approve of her choice or not, things are what they are." I told him I understood. He told me, "Things do not always work out the way we want, but life is funny like that." After that we spoke no more of it. Instead we fished, talked, and we enjoyed the day. We stayed out longer than most of the other guided fishing trips. It was as though he did not want to go back, but finally we embarked on our journey back to the lodge.

We were greeted at the boat dock by Sarah's husband Daniel. "How did you two do? Have any luck?" Sarah's father boasted about our catch and how no one knew the lake like he did. We all had a laugh. I then helped clean the fish with Sarah's dad. Later that evening I retired to my room. I cleaned up and went downstairs for dinner. I had no contact with Sarah that night, except to see her work the other side of the dining room. The contact I was having was in my imagination. In my mind, she was my wife and that was my son. I was living and working at the lodge as her husband, but it was only a dream. It was a dream that will never come true.

The next day I went to see my land. I walked the entire portion of my property along the lake front. I was looking for the perfect place to build a house. I have built this house in my head over and over again. I could never live here full time, but I could fly in from time to time to get away from the reality of the real life that I was living. I found a local architect and we spent six hours going over what I wanted.

It was a twenty-four hundred square foot house with a two car garage. I wanted it three hundred feet from the lake, complete with a covered boat dock. The outside of the house was to be covered in stone; a type of pinkish granite. He told me, it will be costly, but I didn't care. I also dreamed of a large wrap-around porch where I could enjoy the view from where ever I wished. However, my most unusual request was a secret passage way leading from my bedroom down to within one hundred feet from the lake. I made it very clear that an outside contractor was to do the work within the passage. There was to be a ten foot by twenty foot room for storage of valuables. The passage must be fire proof and undetectable to the outside world. To show him I was serious I gave him a package with one hundred thousand dollars cash as a retainer. He gladly took the money and agreed to begin working on the project. I told him that I wanted a rough draft in two weeks so I could look over them before I have to leave town. He asked, "What do you do for a living?" I told him, "I do well, and that was all you need to know." He responded by saying, "Yes sir!"

I spent the next few weeks fishing, relaxing, meeting with the architect, my lawyer, taking care of some banking, and cherishing every moment I could spend with Sarah no matter how small. The day before I left the architect and I finalized the plans for the house. I made sure that the money he needed was made available to him through my lawyer. I told them they could not contact me nor did I know when I would be able to contact them; just to proceed to the best of their ability.

After dinner that evening Sarah came to my room. She asked me, "Why didn't you tell me that you are leaving tomorrow morning?" I told her, "I thought it was best that I just leave." She blurted out, "Do you not realize that I still love you? Even though I cannot have you, *I still love you!*" She then ran from my room.

The next morning when I checked out there was no sign of Sarah. It was probably best this way. When I arrived at the airport I booked a flight to Saint Louis. When I arrived there I rented a car and drove to my mother's farm.

I parked out of the way where I would not be spotted. I just sat and watched. From my vantage point I could see most of the farm. I saw my mother outside hanging up clothing on the clothes line. I saw one of my brothers on a tractor heading towards the back of the farm. I was tempted to go to the house and see my mother, but what would I say? What would I tell her about where I have been? What I have been doing? I thought it was best that I did not, at least not for now.

I sat for a few more moments then like clockwork I saw the mail carrier. She was always there between 11am and 11:30am. I knew my mother would be coming to get the mail by 1:00pm. I drove to the mail box and I put a small box wrapped in brown paper along with a letter I had prepared inside. The box contained twenty-five thousand dollars. Money I am sure my family could use. After that I drove back to the St. Louis airport and caught a flight straight to Langley, West Virginia.

On Sunday I called in as always, "Hello, This is Speedy Glass; we fix your glass in a flash." I responded as always. "This is the Butcher; I am having a meat sale. Are you interested in any meat?" After the proper response and having been connected to a secure line, they offered me another assignment. This one was going to be my pleasure. The target was a retired American living on one of the Virgin Islands. His name was John Swagart. I am not sure what the CIA's problem was with him, but that really never mattered to me.

I arrived at the Virgin Islands in early November. I spent eight days watching, following, and trying to establish his habits. His only for sure habit were that five out of eight days, he walked along the beach at the same time usually around one or two hours before sunset. He was always alone, always the same time, and the same place. That made him vulnerable. This made him a creature of habit; as are all people. The habits we have make us weak.

I decided to start walking the beach every day until our paths cross. The first day I walked the beach in the same general location as he did, hoping to run across him. The second day ended the exact same. On day three I was walking and suddenly there he was walking alone. Not many people were around either. The beach was semi private. I walked up to him and said, "Nice day is it not sir?" He replied, "Yes it is. Are you an American?" "Yes I am, and you?" He told me, "I am a retired American businessman and that I moved to the Virgin Islands to live out the remaining years of my life. My wife passed years ago and my only son has not spoken to me in years."

We then walked together for a few moments. After I was sure no one was around I simply snapped his neck then threw his body in the ocean. I walked back to my car and returned to my hotel room. I spent the next week on vacation. This was a *truly* beautiful place.

It was almost December when I arrived back at Langley. For the next few months things were quiet. I spent my time at the gym working out, mastering martial arts, brushing up on foreign languages, and always had time to spend at the shooting range. I tried to always stay prepared for whatever came my way.

CHAPTER THIRTEEN

In early February, 1972 I was summoned to eliminate a problem in Israel. I was to go there under an assumed name as a tourist on a pilgrimage. I would take tours during the day to see things such as, the birth place of Jesus, the Wailing Wall, and enjoying the culture. My target was a Rabbi name was Joseph Katz. He was a holy man. Revered and respected by many.

As usual I took my time finding out all I could about my target. He lived a simple life. He was always in his room for a nights' sleep by 9:30pm every night without fail. I let myself into his dwelling and hid myself in his closet until the time was right. I was supposed to kill him with an Arabic made dagger and make it appear as if someone in the Arabic world had killed him.

As he came out of his bathroom I was hiding behind a large chest of drawers. As I prepared to kill him with the dagger he said, "Are you right with god?" I said nothing. He once again said, "Are you right with god? It is ok. You can come out. I know that you were sent here to take me home and that is ok, but you must ask yourself are you right with god? For the master you serve cannot save your soul. I except my fate and have anticipated if for quite some time, but again I ask you. Are you right with god and do you think spilling my blood will get you into the kingdom of heaven or will it damn your internal soul?" He then closed his eyes titled his head back and said, "Lord I give unto you my sole for eternal salvation and life." At that moment I drove the dagger into his heart. I found that whole experience to be very strange and very bazaar. I did not hang out in Israel for very long. I was on a plane the next day and on my way back to Langley.

I thought a great deal about what the Rabbi had said how a man cannot serve two masters. One on earth and one in heaven I considered the fact that my eternal soul was dammed and that if there was a God, that he made me and with the knowledge he has, he had to know what he had created. So, maybe he in his wisdom every so often created someone such as me. Maybe I was to show humanity the difference between good, bad, evil, and self-righteousness. The theoretical and theological conversation I was having in my head with myself was starting to give me a headache. In the end the lord can decide if I was a child of God or a disciple of the Devil. All I know is, it is what it is and things are what they are.

A few days after my return to Langley I was contacted by Mike Walters. He wanted to have a meeting with me, as well as a member of the Federal Bureau of Investigations. I inquired as to the nature of the meeting. He stated, he didn't want to get involved in the conversation until we meet. I agreed. We were to meet at a neutral location, the city park. This location was an hour and a half drive from Langley.

We met in the park at a prearranged location and time. I was there two hours early so I picked a spot where I would not be seen, but yet I could see the parking lot as well as the meeting point. My own paranoia made me extremely cautious at times. Mike Walters pulled up first. He was forty-five minutes early. He was also being understandably cautious. Twenty-five minutes, before we were to meet two men pulled up and proceeded towards Mike Walters. They spoke briefly. The younger of the two walked away. He kept himself at a safe distance. I was not sure what was going on, so I removed my pistol from its holster and put it in my left pocket. The last thing you want to do if you are right handed, such as myself, is put it in your right pocket and upon meeting someone have to release it to shake their hand. This left you vulnerable to what we in the trade call a "deadly hand shake."

I headed off towards them. The weather was cold and crisp. It was after all, late February. As I approached them, not knowing what I was walking into, they spotted me. They watched me cautiously as I approached. Finally, I was upon them and just as I had expected Mike Walters introduced the agent from the Federal Bureau of Investigations to me as Agent Terry Nash. I took my right hand out of my coat pocket said, "Hello." I then said to him, "Let's see some identification." He asked, "Are you serious?" I told him, "Serious enough that if you do not produce some identification that I am prepared to end the meeting." He reached for his identification and at the same time stated, "You are not a very trusting soul, are you?" I told him that if I were to blindly trust people on their word, or faith I would not be here today. Don't take it personally. I consider it to be a good business practice." He told me, "No offense was taken." Then Mike Walters spoke, "David, the reason we have asked you to attend this meeting is because the Federal Bureau of Investigation with the cooperation of the CIA, as well as your country, needs your help." I asked, "Exactly what is it that everyone needs from me?" Mike Walters felt it was best that Terry Nash explained the situation.

Mr. Nash started by telling me that he was the head of the FBI. It was his job to investigate and bring down organized crime in the United States. He proceeded to tell me that Mike told him after a conversation that they were having about the problems associated with trying to get someone on the inside to collect information that would bring these people down, that he might have someone who could help. He told me you are a *made man* in the Tortanallia crime family out of Chicago even though you have since left I understand it was under circumstances that may make it difficult to return. I thought that if we put our collective thoughts together we might be able to come up with something. Even though this would be a long shot what do you think?" I told him, "I think we need to go someplace warm to conduct this meeting , and the next time we meet make sure you come alone. You and your friend over there can leave now. I will talk to Mike and we will set up another meeting." Mr. Nash smiled and said, "Very good and I hope to be seeing you soon."

Mike and I stayed there for another fifteen minutes or so talking about exactly what the FBI wanted from me and what his thoughts were on the situation. We decided to sleep on it and get together in a couple of days to set up a new meeting to discuss our options. Just as planned Mr. Walters called and we set up another meeting at an apartment the FBI used as a safe house when moving people in the witness protection program.

This was much better, it was warm and I could relax a little bit. Now I had time to consider my options and come up with a solid game plan. We all met at the apartment, Terry Nash started the conversation. He felt that I should just go back to Chicago and tell them that there were things that happened and I wished they hadn't, but they had and that I had been in the military since I left. He wanted me to tell them that my loyalty was and would always be with the family. I asked, "Can I speak freely?" He said, "That is what we are here for." I told him, "You are a fucking idiot, and why don't I just shoot myself in the fucking head right now and save "Big Tony" the trouble. Mike told me I needed to calm down, that we are just bouncing ideas off each other and that there was no reason to act that way. I informed the both of them that it was my life they were playing with, not theirs, and that there is only one way I would have any chance to live through the initial meeting. The only way I would make it was to bring a *large* cash gift. I think two million dollars should do it. Terry chimed in saying, "No way the FBI going to give you two million dollars." I told him, "I am not finished. There has to be a hook, some way to make me more valuable alive than dead. I have given this a great deal of thought. *Heroin* is the hook." They both wanted to know what I meant by that. I told them both that with the help of the CIA I could establish an unlimited supply of heroin from the golden triangle in Asia. Supplying them with low cost heroin guaranteed they would make millions. They would probably not kill me and if I could deliver this to them. The CIA could bring the heroin into the country and I would set up a distribution network from coast to coast, not just the Tortanallia crime family and the other Chicago crime families but *all* the major crime families in the country.

Mr. Nash told me, "You have lost your mind." Mike sat saying nothing. I also added as a bonus, "The money being made could be split between the CIA, FBI, and me. I am sure there is always some operation that you two need to fund without the sanction of the United States government." Mike saw the potential, but Terry on the other hand thought we were both crazy. Mike told him that he thought it would work, however only the three of us could ever know the whole story.

By now Terry was considering it a viable plan. I told both of them, "It had to be a long term commitment. Five to ten years, and this is the only way you can achieve your goal. Not to mention I had conditions, first of all I would never testify, not ever, and that "Big Tony" would never be charged for anything." Terry wanted to know, "Why hands off Big Tony?" I told him, "For my own personal reasons." He also thought that I was asking for too much money. I told him, I was the only one risking my life for the next decade and beyond. That *I* was the only one who could deliver to the FBI want they wanted, and that was organized crime on a silver platter.

Throughout the entire sting from time to time you will be supplied information allowing you to bust key members of the major crime families. Like a cancer over time, we could eat them alive. He was definitely interested now, but he had some conditions of his own.

Terry Nash wanted me to take an undercover agent with me. I resisted at first, but then agreed as long as I approved of the agent that he had in mind. He then told me, "The agent I had in mind is outside in his car waiting for the signal to come up."

"You fucking pricks," I exclaimed! "You two had already decided that you were going to make me use one of your people even before we discussed it as a possibility." He replied by saying, "Your god damn right! No matter what the plan I need one of my own on the inside to document times, places, and events." I told him "Fine, but before you bring him up you must understand something. I also have full immunity because I will break the law by committing felony after felony to get you what you want. I may even have to kill. So are you prepared for your agent as well as me to commit crimes, and I mean serious crimes, so you can have what you want? Are you prepared to turn a blind eye to what we do because to be convincing in their world you have to be one of them. Well, what's your answer? Terry paused for a moment and then said, " Yes, but you understand me if this thing gets out of control, the wrong people find out, or if it is just not paying off in dividends like it should be I will pull the fucking plug so fast your head will spin. Do you understand me?" I told him, "I do and you can now bring up super cop."

He walked to the window and opened the shades twice then closed them twice. I laughed. He wanted to know what was so funny. I told him, "You two guys kill me with the cloak and dagger shit." Neither one of them thought it was as funny as I did. There was a knock at the door. When I opened there he was. He looked like a cross between a State Trooper and a Marine drill instructor. I at once knew the wise guys would spot him even faster than me. I told both Mike and Terry both right in front of super cop, "No, not him." They both asked "Why not?"Terry proceeded to tell me that he handpicked him. He was single, no ties and had volunteered for a potentially dangerous mission without knowing what it was. Hell, he still does not know what it is. Don't you at least want to interview him? I said, "Alright what's your name?" "Paul Skoleto" I thought, give me a fucking break. This prick was pure Angelo Saxon. Not a chance did he have any Italian heritage. Paul definitely was not his real name. On to question two, "What kind of gun do you carry?" He showed me, so I naturally asked, "Can I see it?" That prick was stupid enough to hand me his gun, so I decided it was time to find out his real name.

I hit him on the left side of his face with his own gun then I grabbed him by the top of his head and with my left hand I placed the gun to his head. Right about then Terry was freaking out. He pulled his gun on me and told me, "Release agent Skoleto now!" I told him, "Go fuck yourself." I told agent Skoleto, "Give me your real name or I will pull the trigger." Terry Nash was still screaming, "*Release him now!*" The prick told me that his name was Paul Skoleto. At that point I slid the gun to the top of his head and pulled the trigger.

The bullet parted his hair as it grazed past his head. Mike grabbed Terry 's arm just as the gun went off. I'll ask again, "What is your *real* name?" I put the gun to the left side of his nose and said, "In five seconds I will have your name or your brains on the fucking wall behind you." Well apparently they did not teach shit like this in the FBI training manual, even to those at the top of their class because he blurted out, "Paul Anderson. Are you fucking happy. My name is Paul Anderson." I stepped back emptied his gun and gave it back and told him, "Never give up your weapon." Terry was screaming at me, "You crazy son of a bitch! What the fuck is wrong with you? I could have killed you." I replied, "I knew that." He replied, "God damn it. I thought you were going to kill him." I then told him, "At one point I thought I was going to kill him myself. Find me someone I can work with and take Mr. Anderson someplace where he can change his pants." At that point, Nash and Walters looked at Anderson to see that he had pissed his pants and I believe that it was then that Anderson himself realized that he had pissed in his pants.

I told both Nash and Walters, "Find me someone with Italian heritage, no family, no current girlfriend, close to my age, and balls of steal because he will need them." It was then that we heard the police sirens. Someone must have called in because of the gun shots. We decided to leave and they told me that they would contact me.

Six weeks had passed with little to no contact with Nash or Walters except to say that Nash was still searching for someone that they thought I could work with. Finally in April 1972, Mike Walters contacted me to let me know that Terry Nash himself and hopefully my partner wanted to meet with me. We were to meet at an abandoned railway depot in Newbury, Virginia. This time, even though I was one hour early, the other three men were already there. When I came in to the depot there stood Terry Nash, Mike Walters, and the new guy. The first thing I noticed is that he did not look like a cop. Terry Nash introduced him to me as Nicholas Ginato. He took my hand and said, "Call me Nick." Now he looked Italian, he had dark hair and slightly olive skin. His age seemed close to mine. He was six foot tall, two hundred to two hundred ten pounds, and he had not shaved in a few days. He wore blue jeans, a black t-shirt and a denim jacket. He looked the part, but did he have what I was looking for.

Before I could question him Terry asked me for my gun. He said, "I do not want an incident like the last time." I just smiled and laughed. I said to Nick, "Tell me something about you." He said "My parents both died in a car crash when I was twelve and I stayed with my grandma. She died when I was nineteen, so I joined the Marines and went to Vietnam. I came back in one piece and applied with the FBI. I was accepted and I volunteered for undercover work. That's about all there is." I circled around him while he talked. He stood still, not turning his head to follow me as I circled him.

I reached into my leather jacket between my shoulder blades where I had attached a sheath for carrying a knife. As I went by him, while directly behind him, I pulled the knife with my left hand and grabbed the hair on the front of his head. I quickly reached around with my right hand, putting the blade to his throat and asked, "Nick what's your real name?" He answered, "Nicholas Ginato." I told him that if he did not tell me the truth he was dead. He told me, "Do me the favor," and pressed his neck against the knife. I then removed the knife from his neck, put it back in the sheath, and said, "He will do."

As I turned back to Nick he punched me in the face and told me, "The next time you put a knife against my neck you better finish the job." I was on the floor on my ass. Nash and Walters were trying to make sense of things. I put my hand out and Nick helped me up. I looked at him and smiled. I told him, "Like I said, you will do. Now if you gentlemen don't mind Nick and I need to spend some time alone getting to know each other and go over things as I see them." I told Mr. Nash I considered this to be our last meeting. From now on you can go through Nick and Mike you and I can talk more at length later, but for now I want to be left alone with Nick. I suggested we go some place to get a cup of coffee, have lunch, and talk. We went to a local diner, ordered our meal, and started the process of getting to know each other.

We talked about Vietnam. We had to have common stories involving each other in case we were questioned, and we would be questioned. Once that was taken care of I asked him, "Have you realized that there is a good chance that neither of us will live through this?" He said to me, "I look at it like Vietnam. If it happens, it happens. I am not going to give it much thought." I asked him, "Why did you volunteer for an undercover job without knowing what it was?" He said, "I didn't care what the job was. I missed the adrenalin rush that I experienced in Vietnam. I have no family to speak of and I was not in any serious relationship. I just didn't want to be tied to a desk with a suit and tie like Terry Nash. So, I figured that undercover work would suit me best." He then asked, "What is the job?" I told him how we were going to establish the biggest heroin ring anywhere ever and we would base our operation out of Chicago.

He wanted to know how it was going to work. I told him, "You will never have knowledge of how the heroin gets into the country. That information is for me only and the rest we will discuss later. We have covered enough ground for one day. I will contact you in a few days." Before he left I asked him, "Would you have let me cut your throat?" He said, "You had the upper hand and I had no way to stop you. I refused to be a coward. I would rather go out like a man, so yes I would have let you before I told you anything." Alright then, like I said I will contact you in a few days.

After leaving I contacted Mike Walters so we could set up a meeting for the next day to go over the heroin distribution. We met at a local place. When we met the first thing he wanted to know is, "What do you think of Nick?" I told him, "He seemed to have balls of steal, but there is no way to know how he will react until the time comes. On the other hand he seems to be what I was looking for. Only time will tell for sure." Next topic of discussion is about how the heroin would be brought into the country and how the delivery was going to be made.

The heroin would be brought into the country by the CIA courtesy of the United States Military. The crates would be marked property of the United States Government, do not open, and handle with care. The crates would be loaded by the CIA and then unloaded by the CIA. A CIA agent would travel with the crates to their marked destination. They would then transport the crates to a location that I would provide when the time came. This set up would give me an unlimited source of heroin into the United States with a guaranteed delivery. Mike said, "I have already been working on the first delivery. It will take place in four weeks and after that we could expect it as often as we needed it with two week's notice." He told me that his people will deliver the heroin to wherever I need it. Nick would be in charge of collecting all of the money. He will give me my share as well as the CIA's share. He would give the FBI's share to Terry Nash. By involving Nick in collecting the money and giving him knowledge of the delivery he would be able to collect information that will be deadly to the organized crime families of this country.

In order to keep the operation running for a long period of time, longer than any operation has ever run, they would be able to bust large numbers of people at once instead of just knowing who is in possession of the heroin at delivery. This will allow the FBI to follow the product and bust the appropriate people at the appropriate time, but not too many, not too often, and always being careful not to draw attention to the operation. This way like a cancer we will slowly eat away at them until there was little to nothing left. I told Mike, I am going to disappear for a few weeks, but I will be back before we were ready to commence with "Operation Poppy." This was the code name they gave it. I suppose because heroin comes from the poppy plant.

Before I left town I told Nick "You have three weeks to get your affairs in order before we embark on the adventure of a life time. In three weeks I will contact you." He wanted to ask me a lot of questions, but again I told him "In three weeks that I will contact you and then we would talk." All he needed to know for now was that he had three weeks left of whatever life he had because after that life as he knew it would never be the same.

CHAPTER FOURTEEN

When I left for my three weeks of peace I knew that the CIA or the FBI would probably be following me, so I took a plane to Northern California with a layover in Colorado; I got off the plane in Colorado and went into the men's room. I put on a fake disguise and walked out of the men's room with my new look. I then went to the car rental counter and under a different identity I rented a car and headed for Cider Falls, Oregon.

Along the way I removed my disguise. I spent one night in a hotel and woke up early so I would arrive at the lodge later that afternoon. By now it was mid July, 1972 and I had been gone from the lake some seven or eight months. When I checked in at the lodge Sarah's mother waited on me. She was pleasant as always, I asked her how she was doing and how her husband was. After a short chat I excused myself to my room, but before I could walk away she asked me, "Do you not wish to know how Sarah is doing?" I paused for a moment not knowing exactly what to say, and then I finally asked, "How is she doing?" She told me, "Sarah is doing okay, she will be glad to see that you came for a visit." She then smiled and walked away.

I found the conversation to be awkward. I went to my room, unpacked, rested, and then came down for dinner. Sarah's husband

Daniel greeted me. He led me to a table where her father was sitting. He said, he thought that I would enjoy his father-in-laws company for dinner. Sarah's father was glad to see me. We ate our dinner and had a good conversation. All the while I was staring at Sarah as she worked the dining room. I must have drunk four glasses of tea just so she would come over to the table and we could make small talk.

She asked, "Have you been to your new house yet?" I told her that I was planning on going there tomorrow. She told me she had driven by the house the other day and it was coming along nicely. Just the sound of her voice and to be able to just see her somehow calmed me. It put me in a peaceful state.

The next day I went to see my lawyer. We reviewed the progress. He said the house would be done in September. The only problem was the secret passage way. He told me that they had to relocate it in the basement. He said that he hoped that is not a problem. I told him that it was fine. We then drove to the house. When I saw the house I was in awe, It was exactly what I wanted. We discussed where I wanted the boat house and the boat dock. I handed him a check for three hundred thousand dollars. I told him, "The next time I was in town we will go over the cost. You just need to get the project done for me and keep up on my taxes. I will contact you sometime before the year's end." I knew that I would only be able to enjoy this place for short periods of time and only from time to time, but that was okay with me. Small amount of happiness was better than no happiness at all.

For the next few weeks I just relaxed, enjoyed the atmosphere, and savored the precious few moments I had with Sarah. Three days before I left I approached Sarah's husband Daniel and asked him, "With your permission and only with your permission I would like to hire your wife Sarah to furnish and decorate my house in my absence." He paused and looked at me curiously, but before he could speak I told him, "If you like you could help her. I am willing to pay ten thousand dollars cash for your services in advance, of course only if that is okay with you." He did not pause after that. Instead he readily agreed with no hesitation. I asked, "With your approval, can I approach Sarah with the same proposal and discuss my taste in furnishings with her?" He said that would be just fine. I thanked him and left the room.

My head was buzzing. This whole idea of having them furnish my house would give me two days to spend with Sarah with her husband's permission. It is amazing what ten thousand dollars can do. How it can blind and cloud someone's judgment, someone like Daniel.

Later that evening I finally had an opportunity to talk to Sarah. She said to me, "I have already talked to Daniel and I think ten thousand dollars is a ridiculous amount of money. It is too much." I told her, "Daniel did not seem to think it was too much. Besides, I could afford it and you will only be taking advantage of me if you asked me for that amount. Remember, I offered that amount. Plus, any amount of money is worth spending time with you. No matter how small the amount of time would be." She smiled and said, "Okay, you win."

We decided that the next day we would drive to the house to get some ideas. All three of us will meet up for breakfast. She had some catalogs that we paged through to get some ideas. We discussed my taste and we all had our input.

After breakfast Daniel had to attend to some lodge business and was unable to go with us to the house. He said, "I will meet you two later today back at the lodge." Sarah and I left to go out to the house. On the way there she put her hand on my thigh then leaned over gave me a kiss on the cheek. She told me, "I missed you." I held her hand the rest of the way. It felt like more like a date then a business arrangement.

When we arrived at the house the workers were busy. People coming and going; things were moving right along. We walked through the house, room by room, while talking about what I wanted or even more about what she thought I should have. After we finished in the house we walked down to the lake to where they had started on the boat house and dock. We then walked down the shoreline of my property and came upon an out cropping of boulders. It was maybe six hundred feet or so from where the men were working on the boat house. As we walked past the boulders Sarah grabbed my hand and led me into a natural pocket in the boulders. We were surrounded on three sides, the only view we had was that of the lake in front of us. No one could see us and we could see no one, though we could hear them working. We were for all intents and purposes concealed.

Once inside this natural pocket formation Sarah began to kiss me. My heart was pounding. One thing led to another and we ended up with Sarah's pants down around her ankles. She was leaning over a small boulder while I took her from behind. It was magnificent, earth shaking, toe curling, unbridled passion. I would have loved for that moment to last forever, but unfortunately with a woman that good in front of you it is only possible to hold out so long. When finished and then we straightened ourselves up, caught our breath, and proceeded to walk back to the house. We made sure not to walk to close as to cause suspicion from the workers. After all, she was a married woman and this was a small community. We made our way back to the car. On the way back to the house we started up again in the car. We ended up pulling over on a logging road and we drove back a few miles then pulled the car off the road. We were somewhat hidden in the trees and this time it was to be a frontal assault in the back seat, her left foot pressed against the back window of the car. She was a wild cat. She was pulling my hair, and praying to the lord, "Oh god, Oh my god." The more she yelled, the harder we went at it until we both collapsed with complete and utter blissful exhaustion. It took some what longer to compose ourselves this time.

Once we were done we just talked for awhile. We talked about anything and everything, but after a few hours we decided that we should be heading back before we were missed. On the ride back to the lodge we talked very little. We once again held hands until we rounded the corner to pull down the driveway to the lodge. We went inside, chatted for a moment, and then went our separate ways after deciding to meet for dinner that evening. This was so that Daniel, Sarah, and I could discuss the progress we had made.

We met for dinner that evening. As they both talked to me about furnishings ideas, all I could do is replay the days' events in my head and think about how clueless her husband was.

The next day Daniel had to take a couple of men on a guided fishing trip, once again leaving Sarah alone with me. We went to see my lawyer. I set it up so that Sarah could furnish my house and my lawyer would take care of the bills. We then visited a neighboring town to look at a couple furniture stores. I was losing interest in the whole shopping experience, so we headed back to the lodge.

On the way back we once again found ourselves on a logging road and once again I experienced sexual ecstasy. When we finished we again sat and talked. Sarah wanted to know, "How do you afford to spend the way you do while working for the government writing research papers?" I told her that I was a trust fund baby. My parents were well off and they had died when I was young. Since I was the only child all their money was put into a trust fund for me the money doubled, then doubled again, while my grandparents raised me. They died, also leaving their money in a trust fund for me. The interest on my trust funds would pay for the house in less than one year. She then asked, "Why do you work?" I told her, "You must understand that as a trust fund baby I had to do nothing for myself. It made me feel useless and the work I do for the government makes me feel useful. My work is important to a lot of people." She said, "I suppose that's why you cannot settle down, at least for now?" I told her, "That is right." She replied, "Even though I do not understand everything, I am okay with the way things are. As long as from time to time you come for a visit. I will be okay until the day comes that you are ready to settle down to a more normal life."

The next day I arose early to go down for breakfast. Sarah waited on me. Daniel was already gone. He had taken some gentlemen fishing. After breakfast, Sarah and I talked. Before I left she wanted to know, "When will you be back?" I could not give her a time. I had no way to know when, if ever. She wanted to know if I could at least try to call sometime. The best I could tell her was, "Because of the nature of the work that I am involved in, if certain people knew about my relationship with her, they could use her to get to me and that she and her son could be put in jeopardy and this is something I would not allow."

We parted with a kiss and a hug. She cried as I left, leaving was always difficult. As I drove away, I did not look back. Only forward towards Chicago and what I had to do. I drove to the airport in Northern California and hopped on a flight back to Virginia, back to my apartment.

CHAPTER FIFTEEN

The next day I contacted Mike Walters. We met to discuss the situation at hand and the exact when, where, why, and how the heroin would be delivered. The heroin was to come in on Military transports in crates. Inside the crates, the zippers on the duffel bags were to be disabled by using an electric soldering iron. It was important that the duffel bags remained sealed from the time they left Asia until the time the heroin was delivered to the customer. There was no need for curious eyes.

Once in the United States the heroin would be loaded in the trunk of a used car, something inconspicuous. Then at a pre-determined location and time the car would be left with the keys in the car above the visor. The car would be watched at a safe distance until it was picked up by the customer. Then the car would be followed to its destination. The customer was to offload the heroin, put the money in the trunk, and then take the car back to another pre-determined location where Nick would retrieve the car and cash. He would then get rid of the car and bring the cash to me.

I was to retrieve the CIA's cost for the heroin and then split the rest between myself, the CIA, FBI, and Nick. Nick was to deliver the FBIs' share and I would take care of the CIAs' through Mike Walters. Mike told me, "In eight days I will have the two million dollars you needed and ten kilos of heroin. After that, when you need more I will place an order. I can guarantee delivery within two weeks."

The one thing that Mike Walters was bothered with was the fact that from time to time I would disappear. He wanted to know, "Where have you been?" I asked him, "What is wrong?" Did your boys loose me in Colorado?" He smiled and said, "What I know does not bother me. It is what I do not know that worries me." I told him, "Where I go is my business and that it was of a personal nature. It is a relationship that I had developed before I went to Vietnam and that from time to time I need a place to go to get away from everything. Besides, look at how much fun you will have trying to find out where I go." He told me, Be careful and as far as where you go, I am a patient man. I will eventually find out what I do not know. Anyway, when the product comes in I will contact you. Just make sure things are ready on your end."

After I had finished with Mike I contacted Nick. He said, "I am beginning to think that you must have changed your mind." I told him, "Not a fucking chance, I am more concerned that you had changed your mind. We need to get together."

Two days later we meet and spent the next four days together getting our stories straight, getting to know each other better. It turned out that we shared a lot of the same experiences in life besides Vietnam. He also grew up on a farm and he also enjoyed fishing and hunting. Nick had a taste for the ladies as well, but most of all we shared the need for adventure. The need we both have for an adrenaline rush was such that the life of an average person could never provide us. The closer to death we could get without actually dying was the ultimate rush.

My only concern was if he could control his need for the rush that he craved. Only time would tell how Nick would perform under the pressure of what we were about to embark on. I told Nick, "In three days I will meet you in Champaign, IL at the Road Side Inn Truck stop and from there we will drive together to Chicago. You have three days to end whatever life you had and be prepared to live the life of a drug dealer. If you are not at the Road Side Inn in Champaign I would understand." He told me, "I will see you in three days, and don't be fucking late."

Just as planned, three days later I pulled into the Road Side Inn truck stop and there waiting for me was Nick. He said to me, "It is nice to see you could make it on time. Glad you did not change your mind." We laughed.

Terry Nash was also there. He gave Nick the ride to the truck stop. Nash thanked both of us told us, "Be careful and good luck." We put his suitcases in the back seat of my Galaxy 500. He asked, "Why don't we put the luggage in the trunk?" I told him, "The trunk contains ten kilos of heroin and two million dollars cash." I was not going to open it any sooner than I *had* to. The drive from Champaign to Chicago is not far. We talked on the way and as we got closer I could see that Nick was getting anxious. Not scared, but anxious. I could tell the difference. I should know because I was feeling the same way.

When we finally arrived in Chicago and Nick wanted to know, "How will we hook up with Tony Tortanallia?" I laughed, "Hooking up with Tony Tortanallia is easy. Getting out of the situation alive is going to be the hard part."

That night we stayed at the Hilton Hotel in downtown. We brought the money and the heroin to the room. More than once I saw Nick looking at the two briefcases, the ones carrying the money and the heroin. I finally asked him, "What bothers you more, the fact that we have two million dollars cash and ten kilos of heroin in the room? Or is it the fact that you have never seen two million dollars cash in your life, nor heroin in any amount and you're curious?" He smiled and said, "It was the fact that he was curious." I smiled back and threw him the keys and told him, "Satisfy your curiosity, so we can go to sleep".

Nick chose to open one of the briefcases containing a million dollars cash first. You could see it in his eyes. He looked like a kid in a candy store. Nick was amazed. He admitted, "I have never seen so much cash." I told him, "If we live through the day tomorrow we both will see tens' of millions of dollars someday and not give it a second thought." He then closed the briefcase, locked it, and then opened the suitcase containing the ten kilos of heroin. "So this is it, this is what is going to get us in?" he asked. "Yes and hopefully keep us alive." I told him. He closed the suitcase then threw me the keys. Nick said, "I hope your right." I told him, I hoped I was too. After that we tried to get some rest, however I do not think either one of us slept very well that night.

The next morning we woke up early. It was time to test my theory. Nick said, "How do you know where to find Tony?" I told him, "Tony will be easy to find." We drove to Tony's car lot on Cherry Street. I told Nick, "Here goes nothing, or everything." We both exited the car and simply walked into the building like it was just another day, and we were just two guys there to see old friends. One of Tony's boys spotted me. I saw him go to Tony's office. Tony came crashing out. He walked up to me and said, "You are either the stupidest man I ever met or the bravest man I ever known. Which one is it?" I told him, "It depends on how this works out." He asked, "Why would you come back? You know what has to be done right? You should have stayed away; you know what has to be done."

I then heard a car pull up. It was Duke along with a couple of the other boys. Duke walked in, pulled out his pistol, and said, "Tony please, let me please, fucking let me." Tony told him, "Not here, Duke." Nick had a pistol to his head also. He stood carefully still, but calm. I told Tony, "If you hear me out and make a discussion based on business not our old history, I believe that you will agree killing me would be bad business for everybody." At that point Tony nodded to Duke and the other boys. They put their guns down. "Go ahead," Tony said.

I walked over to a desk and laid one of the briefcases on it. I then opened it and motioned for Tony to come over and take a look. After he looked down at the money he turned and looked at me and said, "Is this to wash away your sins toward the families?" No; not just this, but much more. This is a gift for you.

Tony said, "Albert Giania would not be so inclined to forgive the whole "Johnny Jingles" incident." I told Tony, "It is true. You could keep my gift and kill us. You would have gained something and probably make Albert Giania happy. If you will put emotions aside and set a meeting between myself and Albert, I believe I could convince everyone why they should not kill me. Instead they should do everything in their power to keep alive. That is all I have to say about it for now."

Duke spoke up, "Fuck him, and end it right now Tony." Tony stood silent for a few moments then he sighed and said, "I will set up the meeting with Albert. We will keep your friend, and Duke will be with you until the meeting. Do you understand?" I told Tony, "That will be fine. You will not regret this." He said, "For your sake, let us hope so."

Duke and I went back to his bar and waited for the phone call. Duke didn't have much to say except, "I hope I get the opportunity to put a bullet in your fucking head. I knew Eddie since he was a child. I knew his family. He was like a nephew to me and you left him in the fucking woods where he could be chewed on by wild animals before he was found." I told Duke, "I was left with very little choice and whether you believe it or not I didn't enjoy what I did Eddie was a friend of mine too."

We sat and waited. Four hours later the call came then Duke, two of his pals, and I piled into the car. I was behind the wheel. We drove onto a pier on Lake Michigan. Duke instructed me to pull the car into the abandoned looking warehouse.

When we pulled in there were already people in there. I spotted Nick, they had worked on him. He was not looking good. I spotted Tony and Albert next. There were a dozen or more men there all prepared to do whatever Tony and Albert wanted. As I approached the men Albert spoke, "You have your fucking meeting now. Say what you have to say and then I and I alone will decide whether or not you live or die. Now get on with it."

I threw Duke the keys to my car, "Open the trunk and bring me the briefcase and the suitcase inside." He looked at me, and then Tony and Albert both nodded. Duke retrieved the briefcase and the suitcase. He laid them both on the hood of the car. I opened both of them while telling Albert that the money was a gift for past indiscretions but the heroin is the real reason I am back." He looked at me and said, "Explain yourself."

I told them that after I left Chicago I joined the Marines that is where I met Nick. He's the one that your guys decided to work over. We spent a couple of years in Vietnam together. I trust him with my life and likewise. While over there I started selling heroin to the troops. The money was pretty good and the heroin was easy to acquire. After awhile I started to move small amounts at first to other countries, Germany, France and Austria. The money was getting better. When I got out of the Marines I went back to Europe so I could strengthen my connection and my methods of delivery. Nick got out of the Marines and went to work for me. He has been with me ever since, but if I want to make the kind of money that I know is out there I have to get involved in the United States market. I have an endless pipeline of heroin coming out of the golden triangle in Asia with a fool proof method of delivery. And that is where you and Tony come into play. I will supply an endless amount of cheap heroin from Asia to the United States and you two will help me to market it by putting me in touch with the right people from around the country and for that you will receive a percentage of every kilo sold. What we are talking about here today gentlemen is tens of millions of dollars for each of you per year. You can kill me and end it all now or you can guarantee yourself an endless cash flow. The ball is in your court gentleman.

    Albert told me, "You have my attention, but you must tell me what I need to know, and what I need to know is exactly how your pipeline works. Who is your contact? How do you get it into the country undetected? What makes you think your method is any better than the methods tried in the past? These things I need to know. These things I *must* know."

    I told them both, "Albert; Tony I mean no disrespect, but I will never tell anyone who my contact is or how I get the product into the United States. Not even my number one man Nick knows the answers to those questions nor will he ever know. The fact that I am the only one with that information is the only thing that keeps me alive. It is my insurance policy and it's the reason that you two will go out of your way to keep me alive. All you two need to know is that I will guarantee the delivery of the product any place in the United States with two weeks' notice. With the contacts that I make in every major city in this country or elsewhere, you two will receive your cut in cash or free product. I will sell you the product for twenty five percent less than you currently pay.

If we cannot come to an agreement here today then let one of these pricks pull the trigger, but if not then take your first ten kilos of product and let my friend Nick loose."

Tony and Albert walked off to the side for several minutes. They talked, they gestured, and they finally finished. They walked back to where I was. Tony did the talking this time. He said, "David you caused a lot of problems when you left. You took out "Johnny Jingles", you took out Eddie, but this is our business. It is the life we choose or the life that chooses us. At any rate had you not taken Johnny down he would have eventually taken you down. And Eddie, I saw him grow up, but if he had not made a mistake we would not be talking today. And the fact that you came here like a man with hat in hand, bearing gifts of atonement, asking for forgiveness, and prepared to die if necessary tells both Albert and me that you are a man of honor. You must have balls of steel. So we want to put the past behind us, where it belongs, we are prepared to do business with you.

"They then both embraced me with a kiss on either cheek. I said, "You think your boys could let Nick go now Tony?" He then gave a nod. They released Nick and he fell to one knee. I looked at Tony and said, "Was that really necessary?" Tony said, "No, it was not. It was done without my permission."

As I knelt over to help Nick, I saw George Fredmen behind me to the right. He smiled and said, "No hard feelings. I was just trying to get him to tell me something, anything." Nick mumbled into my ear, "I did not tell him one fucking thing." I became very angry. As I stood up I spun around and hit him in the throat with a judo chop. I hit him as hard as I could. The blow knocked him on his ass. He was gasping for air. Within a few minutes he was dead.

Everyone was freaking out. Guns were being drawn. Tony said, "Why, fucking why? You, crazy bastard, what the fuck have you done?" I told Tony and everyone in the room, "If anyone for any reason, at anytime, ever touches Nick, I will die trying to seek revenge. This man saved my life more than once in Vietnam and that I should already be dead, so do not ever believe I am afraid to die. Do we understand each other?"

Albert told Tony, "God damn. We have got a tiger by his tail. You keep him in line. I am making him your problem Tony, not mine and if you cannot handle that, just give the word and we will end it right now." Tony looked at me, then at Nick, and then at the dead man, George Freedman, he told Albert, "I will take responsibility for him."

"See that you do," Albert barked back. His men took the briefcase with one million dollars and half of the product on their way out. I asked Duke if he could help me put Nick in the car. He just nodded and helped me. I told Tony that we would get together in a few days and make plans for delivery so we could market the product. He said, "That will be fine. You know that you are one crazy son of a bitch. Don't ever do something like that around me again. There is a time and place for those things and here was *not* it. You need to work on your self control. Do you understand me?" I told him, "I do." And I started my car and drove away.

I asked Nick if he need to see a doctor. He said he just needed to lie down and rest for a few days. I guess today, July 17, 1972 would be the first time I have seen a man murdered. I told him that what he saw was not murder, it was business. If I had allowed George Freedman to get away with beating you, I as well as you would have been perceived as weak, and if the perception that people have about us is one of weakness, then neither one of us would last very long. I told you what kind of life you were entering into so this should be no surprise. Are you having second thoughts?

"No," Nick replied." I guess I knew that I would see these things, but I was not prepared to see it on the first day. While we are talking, who was "Johnny Jingles?" Was he another business related problem?" I told him, "Yes, he was a problem that I had to take care of before he took care of me. You need not concern yourself with that. It is not your problem, nor your business. You just need to concentrate on getting better and by the way I was impressed with the way you handled yourself." He said that he was impressed as well as shocked by what happened. I told him, "The next time I will try to give you notice if possible."

"I would appreciate it if at all possible," Nick said with a chuckle.

CHAPTER SIXTEEN

When we arrived back to the hotel Nick showered and I had room service bring him something to eat. I told him I was going out for awhile to look some of my old contacts up." He said, "I guess if I inquire to exactly where you are going you will not tell me will you? I simply replied, "No." I then told him, "I will see him later," and left the room.

Well I didn't *exactly* lie to Nick. I was really looking up some old business contacts. I was headed for the devils pit to see my old pal Jason. I had some unfinished business with him. He was the one I bought the twelve-gauge from that I used to take out "Johnny Jingles" and his henchmen.

Jason told some Giania family members that he had sold me the shot gun. That coupled with the fact that Johnny had a beef with me led them straight to me. That is what led Tony to send Eddie and me to Los Angeles supposedly to work with the extended family out there. Now that I was back I could not let him go unpunished. He has to be dealt with.

I knew that I had to act fast. Once he found out I was back in town and that Tony and Albert were not going to take me out, but to the contrary we were in business together. I was not worried, but if I didn't act now I would be empowering him and weaken my own position. If

I believed he was coming after me and didn't act, I would be seen as weak, no matter how you look at it. Jason has to be dealt with.

I drove to the Devils Pit. I passed by very slowly and spotted Jason behind the bar. This was good, he hadn't heard yet. If he had heard, he had not left town yet. I parked just over one block away where I could see the front door in the hope that if he left I would see him leaving. I sat for two and half to three hours watching people come and go. Finally they turned the outside lights off and put the closed sign in the window. It was time to move.

I exited the car, walked across the street, and between two buildings down the alley to the back of the devils pit. I went to the back door it was locked. I made a short walk around to the kitchen and let myself in, with my pistol drawn, and fitted with a silencer. This is a familiar scenario to me. I worked my way towards the bar. As I approached I could hear two, maybe three, men talking. I paused and hid in the shadows of the kitchen which had been closed already. I wanted to hear what they had to say. It might be information I could use later. I could not clearly see the men and I needed to make sure Jason was one of them.

The one man was getting loud. He was agitated about something. I moved as close as I could without being discovered. At that time I realized the man who was agitated was Jason, I had him. I knew I could take the shot, but not yet. I need to know why he is so worked up. They kept moving and went to the other end of the bar, closer to the kitchen. I could now hear them very clearly. Jason was telling the other two men that he was leaving town that very night. He already found out that I was back in town. I heard him say, "You do not understand. Cavanaro is back in town and from what I hear the Giania family and the Tortanallia Family are ok with him. If I don't get out of town it will only be a matter of time before he figures out that I was the one who told that I sold him the shot gun. Once he knows that, he cannot let me live. I am telling you I know the type of man he is no way will he let this go. I am out of here with as much money as I can pull together. There is enough in the briefcase over there to get by for a few years. When I get to where ever I am going, to will contact you guys. You two take care of the place. Just send me a little money from time to time and when he comes around say that you have not seen me in weeks and you do not know where I am. Maybe after awhile I can work something out and come back. Well I am headed out the back door, parked my car on the street behind there earlier today."

The other man spoke, "Let us walk you out." They were headed right toward me. When they were about fifteen feet away I stepped out of the shadows with my gun in position prepared to fire. I put one shot in the head of the man on the left, one shot into the head of the man on the right, and then I drew down on Jason.

He had his hand on the butt of his pistol, the one that was tucked into the front of his pants. I told him, "Take your hand off that pistol Jason. Get back up to the bar, take a seat, and put your hands on the bar behind you." He did exactly as I told him. He started, "Cavanaro, you do not have to do this. You do not understand. They were going to kill my family and I if they found out I was lying to them. My family Cavanaro, my family, I had no choice."

I just stood silent looking at him or better yet through him. "Look man, just listen to me. I have money there. There is almost two hundred and fifty thousand dollars in that briefcase over there. Take it, just let me live man, just let me live. I can help you. I can be your eyes and ears on the street. I swear I will take care of this mess. No one needs to know. Come on, work with me, please, I am reaching out to you, please?" I asked him, "Are you done?" He said, "Yes, I am done."

I told him "Ok, now it is my turn to talk. You can put whatever spin you want on it. You are the one who fucking ratted me out. I know it and you know it. No matter what you say, you will die here tonight. Make no mistakes about it, consider yourself dead right now. I look at it like you have lived several years more than you should have. I should have killed you after I bought the shotgun from you, but I didn't. That was my mistake. I left a loose end and here I am today. Now I am going to tidy that up."

I then lowered my gun to my right side and I told him that I would give you a little chance, and that is better than no chance. "Reach for your gun Jason, who knows, you might get lucky."

"Come on Cavanaro, don't do that to me."

"I am counting down from ten. On one I will put a bullet in your head."

"Ten…Nine…Eight…Seven…Six…Five."

It was then that Jason made his move. He made a sound that was half whimpering, half crazed anger, as he went for his pistol. He actually had his hand on the pistol and out of his pants before I placed three bullets center mass.

He fell to the floor not quite dead yet. I said, "Well I guess it was not your lucky day." I then picked up my empty bullet casings, grabbed the money, and exited out the back door. When I arrived back at my car I put the money in the trunk and took off back to the hotel.

When I walked in the room I was greeted by Nick pointing a gun at me. I told him, "To calm down cowboy. Go back to bed. It has been a long day." Nick laughed," No shit." Did you have any luck making connections with any of you old contacts?" I answered, "I found who I was looking for that I think things worked out to my advantage. It is two thirty in the morning. I am tired and need to rest. We will talk tomorrow.

That night I was not able to fall right to sleep. The adrenalin rush I felt from letting Jason reach for his pistol jacked me up. I finally fell asleep around four o'clock

At almost ten thirty the next day when Nick started banging on my door yelling, "Wake up. The day is almost over." I jumped up, showered, dressed, and when I came out he was already dressed and ready to go. I told him, "You must be feeling better by now." He said, "I have been worse. Don't you worry about me, I will be just fine." He then asked, "What is on the agenda for today?"

"First thing we need to do is get something to eat." I am starving," I said. He agreed, "You and I need to go someplace where we will be seen." I decided to take him to O'Banions Steakhouse. It was a restaurant favored by, shall we say, men who tend to work outside of the law.

We pulled up to the valet parking, went inside, and we were seated. The waitress came over and we ordered our meals. Right then Adam Antello, a member of the Giania family, spotted me. He got up from his table and walked directly towards me. He did not look happy. When he neared the table he sat down and told me, "You have got balls showing your face in this town. Enjoy your meal. It might be your last."

"Are you done Adam? Now let me tell you something, this is my associate Nick. Not only am I *back* in town, I am bigger than ever and before you do something stupid, you need to get in contact with your people. I have made peace with Albert and Tony. If I were you, I would not want to be the one to tell Albert that you just killed the goose that lays the golden eggs. So, if you don't mind and even if you do you fucking prick, I am trying to eat my lunch, and you are stinking up the place, so go make your phone call. Now get the fuck out of here."

All he said was, "You better hope you are right." He then walked directly to the payphone by the restrooms. Nick and I could see him talking. He was not on the phone long and when he came back to the table he said, "I would like to apologize for this misunderstanding. The meal is on me."

He also told Nick, "It is nice to meet you. I am looking forward to getting to know you." Adam then told me, "There are no hard feelings on my part and I hope there are none for you." I told him that no offense was taken. You had no way of knowing that things had been worked out. The next time we meet; dinner or drinks, whatever, it's on me." He then shook my hand as well as Nick then excused himself.

When he got back to his table we watched all of them while they talked. After a few minutes the two other men with him nodded and raised their glasses toward us. I told Nick, "How do you like that, you and I are untouchable. Anyone who does not know it now, will shortly. Within a few days we will be able to go *anywhere* and do just about *anything* in this town that we want too." Nick just said, "That's all right."

We finished our meals and left. We stopped by Dukes place so I could talk to Duke for a few minutes. I told him, "I want you to set a meeting with Tony and Albert, so that we can finalize our business agreement." Duke told me, "I will contact you as soon as things are set in place." I told Nick, you and I need to find someplace to live besides the hotel that we were staying in. We stopped by a realtors' office and set ourselves an appointment for the next day at ten o'clock in the morning. I asked Nick if he was feeling ok, or if he wanted to go back to the hotel. He wanted to know why I asked, and if I had something in particular in mind. I told him, "If you feel up to it, we could go to a high class whore house that I know of." He laughed and said, "I have never felt so bad that I could not enjoy the company of a woman." We got to the whorehouse at around three o'clock and stayed until almost six o'clock.

Nick and I went to dinner at to the nicest steak house in town. It had been a good day, a productive day. We later returned to the hotel, it was just after nine o'clock. We talked about a few things and watched a little television, and slowly we turned in for the night. I told Nick, "I am going to bed. Call down to the desk for a wakeup call at seven a.m. We have to meet that realtor by ten o'clock."

Just as planned the phone rang at exactly seven o'clock. We showered and dressed. Nick had room service bring us some breakfast and by nine fifty-five we were at the realtor's office. The person they gave us turned out to be a drop dead gorgeous women, she was maybe thirty years old. This is one shopping experience that I would enjoy. She already knew roughly what we were looking for. We wanted two condominiums in the same building. After showing us several, we finally found what we were looking for, two condominiums on the same floor of the same building.

Nick and I agreed and told her we would take them. "How will you be financing them she asked?" I told her, "We will be paying cash." After all we did not have to worry about the Internal Revenue Service, the FBI, and the CIA where running interference for us. She asked me, "Exactly what is it you two do for a living?" I told her, "We do just fine, and we have plans to open a string of gentleman's clubs in the greater Chicago area." I watched for her reaction; she was very calm, very professional. She asked, "Do you need help locating property in the area to build or the right building to buy and renovate?" I told her, "We are interested in obtaining your services for that task." She needed a few days to finalize the paperwork before we could move into our condominiums.

Later that day, Duke contacted me. The meeting was set. We were to meet at Johnny O's night club. It was a popular place where people who had money went to be seen. Time for the meeting was set for at eight o'clock that evening.

When we arrived at the club, we approached the table where Albert was sitting. Albert said, "Your boy can wait over there at those other tables."

"No he will not. He is with me and he is responsible for the delivery of the product and the collection of the payment. He stays or there is no meeting." Albert looked at me with a disappointed look but agreed reluctantly. Nick can sit in on the meeting, but before that happens we need to check the both of you. This was when Duke stood up and patted us both down, not for weapons, but more for wires. When he finished I asked, "Is everyone satisfied?" Tony spoke up, "Don't take it personally. You can never be too careful." Finally we seated ourselves. I asked, "Are we ready to talk business?" Tony said, "Go ahead, lets' hear it."

"To start with, from this point on we will refer to the heroin as "Sugar." We will never again call it by its real name. Once a month Nick will call whoever you want him to deal with, but always the same person for each one of you. When he calls he will say, Hello, This is Mr. Wolf. I am calling to see how your sweet tooth is doing this month. On a scale of one to ten how sweet does your tooth feel? You will respond by rating how you felt on a scale of one to ten. For example; if you want eight kilos, you will simply say that on a scale of one to ten you feel like an eight. Mr. Wolf will then excuse himself from the phone. He will contact you one day before delivery. The place of delivery and method delivery, once established, will never change. The same will apply to the method of payment. There will never be any orders placed for less than five kilos." Upon receiving your first order you both will include enough extra money to cover the first five kilos you received a few days ago. That was not a gift.

Tony spoke up and said, "This was by far the purest product anyone has ever seen. It's almost too pure. Where did you say it was coming from?" I told you, "It comes out of the golden triangle in Asia. That is all you need to know, other than the fact it is a premium product. Albert wanted to know, "How much will we make for putting you in touch with contacts around the country?" I told both Albert and Tony, "You two will both receive five percent from every sale made to a contact that they set me up with. It may not seem like much at first, but as this thing grows your cut will get bigger and bigger every month. Not only will you make money here in Chicago, but you will make money from around the country. The more contacts you give me, the more you make. The more you make, the more we make. The biggest problem we all are going to have is what to do with all that money. How will we transport it, store it, clean it."

Tony said, "I can live with that problem." I then told them, "After tonight you will no longer be able to discuss the product with me. I will work through Nick to minimize my exposure. I suggested you both do likewise." After that Nick and Duke excused themselves from the table to finalize details. Tony, Albert, and I sat, talked, drank and enjoyed the evening.

Albert told me, "You need to get some sort of a legitimate business started." I told the both of them about my plan to start a string of gentleman clubs. They both thought it would be a good idea. Tony asked, "What are you going to name your clubs?" I told him, "They will be called B & B's gentlemen club."

"What does that stand for," Tony asked? I told them it stands for, "Ball Busters." We all had a laugh after that.

Within the week we were living in our new condominiums. Nick collected the money for the first ten kilos of heroin delivered to Tony and Albert. Our journey was just now about to begin.

CHAPTER SEVENTEEN

The first part of August, 1972, Nick took an order from Duke. He needed six kilos. Nick also took an order from Steve Besteto. He was the contact from Albert Giania and he wanted five kilos. The product was moving, the delivery went just as planned, as well as the pay off.

By mid August I was contacted by Tony about going to Detroit to see a man named Joe Bass. I was given a number to call to contact Mr. Bass. I told Tony, "I will call twenty-four hours, before we are to meet, to let Mr. Bass know where the meeting will be held."

Nick and I had spoken at length as how to get the meeting taped, but not to get caught. We finally came up with the idea that the meeting would be held in an athletic club. This way we will make our preparations either before or after hours. The meeting will be held in the steam room with the new client and everyone involved wearing nothing, but a towel to ensure their safety, as well as ours. The point being to guarantee that no one was wearing a wire. Nick and I will have the steam room set up with an audio transmitting device ahead of time. With the meeting place prepared I contacted Mr. Bass. We were to meet at five a.m.

When he arrived, Nick led him back to the locker room. I was there already wearing nothing, but a towel. He had two men with him, they all approached. Mr. Bass began to speak about "Sugar". I explained, "The meeting will be held in the steam room. You and anybody else who wishes to attend the meeting needs to strip down, put a towel on, and join me in the steam room. This way you know I am not wearing a wire and I know you're not." His first response was, "Fuck you. I am not getting naked for anyone." I told him, "That is fine. There will be no meeting and you can continue to pay twenty percent more for your product than was necessary, but I understand." I then excused myself to the steam room.

Within minutes I was joined by Nick, Mr. Bass, and one of his two men. Nick and I went over our system of product delivery and payment. Mr. Bass wanted to deal with Nick, once a month personally. He placed his first order of five kilos and we shook hands.

Ten days later he received the product and we received our payment. Things were looking up; in just over one month we had three satisfied customers.

Early September, 1972, Tony, put me in contact with a gentlemen from Philadelphia, the city of Brotherly Love. His name was Jeff Ross. The same set up was employed, we meet, took to a steam room, he placed his order for five kilos of product, and within ten days he had the product. We received our cash the next day, yet another satisfied customer.

In late September, Albert contacted us through his man Steve Besteto. He wanted us to contact, a gentlemen in New York City. This was the "Holy Grail" of organized crime, his name was Salvador Vincetie. He was the captain in the Vincetie family and will be the one in charge of distribution of the product through New York City streets.

We met in the same manner that I always did. The only request made was that we did not sell any product to anyone else in the state of New York *or* New Jersey. "I told him, I will consider that, but in order to do that he had to make a minimum order of twenty kilos at a time. If not, I was free to pursue other clients in the area." He felt that the amount of product was a bit high, but if it would guarantee him sole distribution rights in New York and New Jersey, he would be willing to purchase twenty kilos. We shook hands and as usual the product was delivered and we received our share.

Terry Nash was excited according to Nick. He was not sure at first that this would work, but not only was it working, it was working better than Nash could have imagined. If only he knew that we had just started.

I decided it was time to get B and B's Gentlemen's club off the ground. I contacted the same realtor who sold us the condos, her name was Cathy Finch. I told her, "I am looking for a building that I could convert into a gentlemen's club." She responded by saying, "A topless bar?" I told her, "You are correct, but I think it sounds better the way I said it." She just smiled and told me, "There will be zoning issues, but I thought we will be able to work that out. Also, I need time to locate the right place. I will get back to you in a few weeks."

It was early October, 1972, when Steven Besteto contacted Nick on Albert's behalf to give us the name of a gentleman in Dallas, Texas. His name was Mark Grant. The meeting was in the usual place, nothing particularly unusual about it. Everything went off without a hitch. He placed his first order of five kilos of product. The delivery went as well as the pay-off, flawless.

The only unusual thing about the trip to Dallas would be the conversation I had with Mike Walters before I went to Dallas. When I told Mike, "I am going to Dallas," he acted slightly strange. I asked Mike what was wrong? Mike responded by telling me, "There is absolutely nothing wrong." I told Mike, "Maybe I was wrong, but I thought that maybe even if for only a second, when I mentioned Dallas, you had a look on your face."

Mike told me, "My daughter lives in Fort Worth, Texas which is not far from Dallas." I told Mike, "Your daughter picked a nice part of the country to live in." I then asked Mike, "Is she married, has she had made you a grandfather yet?" Mike said, "She was indeed married, but she has no children yet." I thought that the conversation about his daughter was over at this point, but he had that look again as if though he wanted to say something more. I once again asked the question,

"Mike, what is bothering you? Just tell me." Mike looked at me he drew a breath as if though he was going to speak, but yet he did not. I told him, "Mike I told you once before that I would kill for you, no questions asked, so tell me whatever it is that's on your mind."

Mike once again drew a breath, but this time he spoke." It is my daughter."

"What is the problem with your daughter," I asked? Mike then told me, "She is in a marriage that she is not happy with." He told me, "My son-in-law cheats on her and tends to drink too much. When he is drunk he becomes both verbally and physically abusive." I told Mike, "Your son-in-law does not seem like a very nice person, at least not where your daughter's concerned." Mike then said, "I don't care for my son-in-law, and my daughter would be better off without him." I then at this point asked Mike, "What does your son-in-law do for a living?" Now keep in mind that Mike could have ended this conversation at any point, but instead Mike told me, "He is the general manager of sales for a Cadillac dealership in Ft. Worth."

Mike told me, "It is the only Cadillac dealership in Fort Worth to my knowledge. Be careful in Dallas, and I will talk to you when you get back." I knew exactly what Mike wanted from me; there was no doubt in my mind.

After our meeting in Dallas I told Nick, "I have an old Marine buddy who lives in Texas and I am going to rent a car and go look him up." Nick wanted to know, how long I would be gone. I told him, "I really wasn't sure, maybe two or three weeks. I need a break, but I will stay in contact."

Nick went back to Chicago and I went to Ft. Worth. I was looking for the only Cadillac dealership in Ft. Worth. I found it with ease. I went inside pretending to be a perspective customer looking for a new Cadillac. I talked to a sales person and asked a few questions. I then told the sales person, "I am just looking and if I have any questions I will come find him."

I spotted the general manager of sales office, then my target. He was sitting at his desk. Now the question was how to handle my target.

There was a parking lot across the street where I parked my car and waited. I knew he would eventually leave and when he did I would follow him.

After several hours had passed he pulled out in his nice new Cadillac Eldorado. I followed him at a safe distance as he drove to a town called Denton. He pulled into a motel, the kind of motel that is off the beaten path, the kind that a person would use to have an affair. I drove by as he turned into the motel and then I turned around. As I came by the second time I saw him go into a room on the first floor. I waited in my car just down the street, from a vantage point where I could see his room.

Just after nine o'clock that night a women left the room, hopped into a car, and drove away. I then exited my car and walked over to where he had parked. When he came out of the room I approached him telling him to open the passenger door. While showing him my gun at the same time I told him, "If you do exactly as I say you will live, but if you don't I will kill you where you stand." He opened the passenger door and walked around to the driver door, unlocked it, and got into the car.

At this point I still had no real plan for taking care of him. I told him to start driving. He wanted to know, "What is going on? Who are you? That wasn't your wife was it? She told me she was not married." I told him, "She isn't my wife. A friend of mine just wanted me to talk to you to explain something and give you a second chance at a better relationship with *your* wife before steps are taken to remove you from the relationship, permanently." He looked at me and said, "You spoke to my father-in-law. He sent you didn't he? Look, he never liked me. I know who he works for and what he can have done if he wants."

At that moment it came to me. I saw a train coming in the distance. There were no cars around, just us. I told him, "Stop the car at the train tracks." He asked, "Why?" We have plenty of time to get across the train tracks. I told him, "Put the car in park. I am in no hurry and I am going to do the talking. I want you to shut up and listen." He put the car in park and shut his mouth.

I started talking to him about family values and whatever else I could think of to occupy him. While I was talking I put the stub nose .38 caliber pistol in my left hand. I then hit him in the forehead with the pistol as hard as I could. His head snapped back then he fell forward. He was unconscious, but still alive. I sat him up, exited the car, walked around to the driver side, put the car in neutral, and gave it a slight push. The car came to rest on the train tracks. The train was within a quarter of a mile now. At sixty miles an hour he would not be stopping anytime soon. I started walking away as the train was blowing his whistle. I turned back to see what I knew was about to happen.

The train hit his car broadside and the impact caused the car to burst into flames. He was dead immediately and it was done in a way that looked like an accident. This way there wouldn't be quite as much stress on his widow. I hiked back to my car and headed for Cider Falls, Oregon.

Along the way I stopped and spent the night in a hotel like usual. The next morning I left early and arrived at my house later that day. The place looked very nice. Sarah did a wonderful job on the furnishings. I was pleased with the way things turned out, but now to see the masterpiece, my tunnel.

I walked down to the basement, accessed the tunnel, and I turned the lights on. I followed it and after going close to three hundred feet, at the end, was a set of stairs. At the top of the stairs was a lever. I turned the lever, unlocking what was above, and I then pushed on the object above me. It swung open and when I came out of the tunnel I was in my boat house. The object above me was the bar. It would swing open to reveal the tunnel or close to conceal the tunnel. I was not sure how much I would use it, or if ever, but I felt better by just having it.

Once back in the house I called the lodge. Sarah answered. I swear at that moment I felt in my heart lump up in my throat. Sarah said, "Hello," for the second time. Finally, I spoke, "Hello Sarah. This is Mr. Roberts." Sara replied, "Is that right? What can I do for you Mr. Roberts?"

I told Sarah, "I will be coming home for a visit the day after tomorrow and I will gladly pay for you to clean the house before I get home." Sarah asked me, "Is that all that you will need from me?" I asked Sarah; "Is your husband or anybody standing by you?" "Yes, that will be fine Mr. Roberts," she replied. I then asked Sarah, "Do you miss me as much as I miss you, and will you be able to tend to all my needs when I came home?"

Sarah then said, "That should not be a problem. I believe I can handle whatever you need." She then said, "Thank you Mr. Roberts, I look forward to seeing you." I told her, "I am looking forward to doing much more than *seeing* you" Then we hung up.

I parked the car in the garage and put everything in my bedroom just in case Sarah came in and I was not ready for her. I wanted to surprise her. I hardly slept, anticipating her arrival.

The next morning I was up out of bed, showered, shaved and dressed by seven o'clock. Time seemed to be barely moving. Eight o'clock no Sarah, ten o'clock no Sarah, finally at ten thirty-five I heard Sarah's car pull up. I peeked out the window and there she was all bundled up with her winter clothing. To me she still looked like an angel. I went into the kitchen and I sat at the breakfast bar waiting for her to come in. I heard her unlock the door taking off her shoes, her coat, and then the sound of her footsteps moving across the floor.

My heart was pounding. She popped out from the around the corner and when Sarah saw me she dropped everything she was carrying and leaped into my arms. She actually knocked me back against the countertop. We looked up and immediately started to undress each other right there on the kitchen countertop. After that we caught our breath and talk for a few moments. We retired to the bedroom for round two which was just as passionate as round one, if not more passionate. Then we laid there for a few hours just holding each other and talking. I am not sure but I believe I can speak for the both of us when I say that we did not want to let go of each other.

Finally at two-thirty Sarah said, "I have to be getting back to the lodge before my husband starts to wonder why I have had been gone for such a long time." I told her, "I will come by tomorrow afternoon as if though I had just arrived in town and act like I just saw the job you and your husband had done furnishing my house." We shared a long goodbye kiss and an even longer embrace before she left.

The next day I went by the lodge around two o'clock. Sarah's husband Daniel greeted me as I came through the door. The first thing that Daniel said was, "Have you seen your house yet?" "Yes I have, it is perfect. The both of you did a wonderful job for me. It was money well spent," I replied. Daniel then said, "Sarah is around here somewhere. She will be glad to hear that you are pleased." Daniel and I then went into the great room where we had a drink by the fireplace. We chatted about meaningless things for awhile and then Daniel excused himself to go find Sarah.

When Daniel returned he was with Sarah and she had their son Michael with her. When they approached Sarah said, "Hello Mr. Roberts. I hope you liked the furnishings in your new home." I told her, "After seeing the house I am more than satisfied." I then asked Sarah with the permission of her husband, would it be ok for me to call on you to clean my house on occasion. Like when I am going to be coming back into town. I am more than happy with what she had done to my house yesterday. I reminded them that I would be willing to pay for her services of course.

Daniel said, "That is fine with me as long as Sarah is ok with it." Sarah said she was fine with the arrangement as well. She said that she enjoyed taking care of things yesterday and that it gave her a break from her daily routine at the lodge.

I believe that this whole cat and mouse game was getting her as sexually excited as it was me. Sarah then excused herself from the room and as polite as you can be Sarah had her son Michael say, "Goodbye Mr. Roberts." He then shook my hand. Michael was a cute child. He had her eyes and dark skin. His birthday was in a few months, towards the end of January. Michael will be turning four years old.

The next day Sarah called me to let me know, "My husband is going on a two day hunting trip so I will be coming to your house to see you tomorrow." Sarah came over we spent a good part of the day relaxing. I told her, "It is unfortunately time for me to be leaving again." Sarah wanted to know, "Where are you going?" I told her, "We have talked about this before and you know I cannot tell you."

"Not even me," Sarah questioned? "No, Sarah, not even you. If I were to tell you of the work that I am involved in, it would put you and your family at risk. That is all I can tell you. Now let's not speak of it anymore. I am leaving in the morning and I have no idea when I will be back."

She did not like that part of our relationship to much, but she knew that she would have to live with the way things were or end what we had all together. Luckily for me she chose not to end things. The next morning I was up, packed and ready to leave early when Sarah pulled in the drive way like she was going to a fire. "Is everything ok, Sarah," I asked? Sarah replied, "No, I could not let you leave without getting one more hug, one more kiss, and I do not want you to say one word. Just make me feel loved right now."

I grabbed Sarah, pulled her tight, gave her a deep long kiss, and a hug that came close to breaking her ribs. When I let go, Sarah smiled, walked to her car, and drove away.

The next day I was back in Chicago. I talked to Nick, things were under control. I called Mike Walter to place a couple of orders. Not once did he mention the trip to Dallas or what had happened in Ft. Worth.

CHAPTER EIGHTEEN

It was early November, 1972 when Cathy Finch called saying she located a couple properties that she wanted me to look at. We set a time and date to take a look at the properties.

Cathy and I met and we looked at several properties the next morning. Nothing really caught my eye until Cathy showed me the last property of the day. It was Cathy's last choice, but I liked it. Cathy said, "The zoning here will not be a problem, but I feel that the property needs too much work."

I had a vision that she did not have or could not have thought of. Cathy thought I just wanted a gentleman's club, but I had other plans. The property was located in a neighborhood that was slightly run down. I wanted to purchase one of the buildings or all of the building that were for sale at the location. So that is exactly what I did, I bought all of the buildings on the entire block. I had just purchased was a one square block of Chicago real estate that was in desperate need of some attention.

I met with an architect in late November, 1972. There were four buildings on the property, the building on the northwest and the southeast corners were to be removed. This would leave a parking space behind each building once which was to become my gentleman's club. The other would become an apartment complex. Once finished the two parking lots would have a six foot rod iron steel fence around them. One parking lot will be for my club and one for the apartment building. Once the architect had finished his plans I then contacted the same contractor who built my house. I simply contacted them saying, "A friend of mine Mr. Roberts has recommended you and I would like you to help me on a project in Chicago."

They arrived in Chicago and we met up at the site. What I wanted from them was for them to restore both buildings to my specifications. The three story building on the southwest corner will be the club, the four story on the northeast corner will be the apartment building, and what I *really* want from you is to make the entire third story of the club my living quarters. Leading from the third story of the club to the corner apartment will be a secret passage. There will be stairs from my living quarters leading to the tunnel. The tunnel will lead to the apartment building and will allow me to come and go without being detected.

No matter what, I will always have an escape route. The third floor of the club will have bullet proof windows, its exterior doors are to be made by a safe making company, and the roof was to be fitted with the latest video surveillance system money could buy, as well as placing cameras throughout the entire club.

Once on the third floor of the club you will pass through a door leading to my office. From there I will be able to see through a two way mirror to the activities at the club as well as monitor the surveillance equipment. Beyond the office was another secure door leading to my living quarters.

Work would begin in the spring of 1973, and was to be completed by fall of the same year. Everything was in place, the money was pouring in, and I had connections in the finance world. For a forty percent fee they would launder my money.

The money was placed in off shore accounts and moved from one account to another. After at least a dozen moves the money would then be wired to my personal account in the United States when I needed it. If I didn't need it I would leave it in one or more of the off shore accounts. The money was clean and virtually undetectable.

It was now March of 1973, Nick and I had set up a meeting in San Francisco. The same tactics were employed for the meeting. Our contact in San Francisco was a man named Mark Ellis. He brought along with him the man in his organization that would be moving the product for him. His name was Jerome Attwel. The meeting was productive and they decided that they could handle eight kilos of product per month.

After the meeting in the locker room, for whatever reason, Nick and Jerome got in to a conversation about how shiny Jerome's shoes were. Nick told him, "They are the shiniest shoes I have ever seen." Jerome told Nick, "They were custom made leather shoes and if you looked close you can see four rows of stitching in the shoes. This is one more row than normal and as far as I knew no one around here makes these shoes this way. Besides, a black man likes to look good." I found the whole conversation to be strange and could not wait to get back to Chicago.

Once I was back in Chicago I could concentrate on finding a location for the next B & B's Gentleman's Club. As promised in the spring of 1973, they started the renovation on the property that I purchased. I met up again with Cathy Finch and we went property shopping once more.

We settled on a property and location that would meet all the proper criteria, zoning, and etc.... This particular property only needed to be altered slightly to prepare for B &B's grand opening. I asked Cathy if she would like to have dinner to celebrate her second real estate sale to me. Cathy told me she thought that we should keep things on a business level and besides with two gentlemen's club you should already have a large selection of women to choose from.

June, 1974, B & B's had its grand opening and the place was packed and all of the women were gorgeous. I have to give credit where credit is due; Tim Hopkins is the man I hired to run my clubs. He has been in the topless business for years. He took care of everything. I will admit that I did sit in on the interviews to hire the girls; that was an intense week. The next club should be open by September, 1974.

I did manage to find time to head back to Cider Falls, in March to see

Sarah, but with the clubs opening and the increasing demand on product it has been hard to get away. Since January 1975, Nick and I have added a client in Atlanta, Georgia. His name was Josh Wilkens. He was joined by a client named Pat Fowler in Seattle, Washington.

The product is selling itself. Nick spends most of his time on distribution and collecting money. Right now the biggest problem is what to do with so much cash. Where to hide it? How to move it? At this point my closest at the condo was full of boxes of money. I never thought having this much money would be so much work, but it is a burden that I could bare.

In less than one year Nick and I were moving forty to fifty kilos of product per month. Terry Nash was like a kid in a candy store. Terry's biggest problem was he had too many people to investigate. The FBI will be busy for years to come with just the information they have acquired already.

CHAPTER NINETEEN

June, 1975, Mike Walters contacted me for a meeting. We met at an out of the way road side diner. Mike was already there when I arrived. I asked him, "Things ok? Why, the secret meeting?" Mike drew a deep breath before he began to speak. He then said, "I need you to take care of something for me." I just nodded yes. Then without pause Mike began to tell me, "Senator Joe Johnson from the fine state of Kentucky. This is the same Senator who sat on the appropriations committee that funds the CIA's missions going on around the world. Sometimes members of congress know what they are giving money for and sometimes they do not. In Senator Johnson's case he knows way too much. In recent days the good senator has been having problems with the IRS, not to mention Congress has been taking a look at him as well. It seems he is on tape and video taking money from large business in order to have some bills passed that would be favorable to them. The house ethics committee is hard after him, heads are about to roll and the CIA is not going to be one of them. Senator Johnson made it clear to the powers at the CIA and FBI that if they do not put pressure on everyone who is after him to let it go, he will not go down alone. Senator Johnson feels that he has served his country well and that his country at the very least owed him the right to a few indiscretions. The powers at be told

Senator Johnson that they would do everything in their power to make things go away, that is where you come in."

"You want me to get rid of a United States Senator," I replied? "That is right," Mike said. "The Senator wanted things to go away and they will. Unfortunately for the Senator he is the thing that needs to go away." I told Mike, "I need to know two things for right now. How much does the job pay and how soon does it need to happen?" Mike asked me, "What do you want to do?" I told him, "I need one million dollars and as much information as you can find on the Senator." Mike agreed to the amount, the information he already had with him.

Mike had everything, the names of his children, where they lived, pictures of his children, grand-children, wife, pictures of the Senator, along with his schedule, and his habits. There were pictures of his mistress, where she lived, her name, and her habits. Laid before me was the Senators entire life as well as the lives of his family.

Mike did insist that I make it look like a suicide or an accident. He also said that I was to do it as soon as possible. I told Mike that I would be willing to do it, but he needed to do something for me. Mike wanted to know what it was that I needed. I told him, "I require the location of the last of the Marines that tortured me in Vietnam." Mike told me, "I feel that you should let it go, just forget about it." He knew I was *not* going to do that. He replied, "If that's what it takes to seal the deal then I will have the information you want in a week or so."

The Senator lived in a rural area of the state. His home was located on a six hundred acre tract of land. It seemed that the Senators hobby was raising pure bred, award winning, quarter horses. I studied his file, looking at every detail, and at every aspect of his life. I studied the aerial photos of his home and property. I knew that the Senator would more than likely be at home keeping a low profile, waiting for things to blow over. I contacted Nick to let him know, "I am taking a few days off and if anyone wants to know where I am just tell them that I went to Virginia Beach with a lady friend of mine."

At this point I had what I needed to take care of the job. I had the location of his house, as well as everything I would ever care to know about him. I believed that I had a solid plan; all I needed to do now was execute it.

I drove to Kentucky then checked into a hotel under an assumed name. The next day was Friday, June, 18th. I took a ride out to the Senators estate. His house was over a quarter of mile off the main road. I circled by the house several times as well as the surrounding area looking for a point of entry into the property. Four miles down the road was Kentucky Lake. I rented a small cabin on the lake under an assumed name and went to town to check out of the motel. Then I went back to the cabin on Kentucky Lake.

The next day I took a hike working my way through the countryside following the tree rows and creeks, keeping myself hidden. When I came upon his property it was still early morning. I found a spot on a hill which was covered with timber. From this spot I could see his house, his stables where the horses were kept, and the surrounding pastures where more horses were being kept. I put my backpack down and then I pulled my thermos out and poured myself a cup of coffee. I made myself comfortable and waited, watching.

At eight-fifteen I saw the senator come out of his house. He sat on the front porch having his morning coffee, reading the paper. No doubt, looking to see what they had written about him today. After thirty minutes the senator went back inside the house and at nine o'clock the senator exited his garage on a golf cart. He was headed for the stables. The senator spent one hour at the stables and drove around his property for another hour, going from pasture to pasture, checking his horses. He then returned to his house. After that I saw the senator two more times just for a few minutes. Each time he came out onto the front porch then went back inside.

The senator from what I had read in his file and what I had seen that day had three hired hands. His file stated that only one hired hand worked on Sunday and he did not start working until eleven in the morning. He only worked long enough to feed and care for the horses. My plan was to be in the stables before sun up. I needed to find a place to hide as well as one where I would be able to see anyone coming.

When I arrived at the stables it was still dark. I quietly waited for the sun to come up. When it finally became light enough to see, I took a look around the stables. There was a landing with a short set of stairs leading up to another set of stairs. Those led up to a hay loft above the stables. I climbed up onto the large pile of hay bales, going back into the stack a few rows, and I removed six bales then repositioned them leaving a pocket in the stack of hay where I was hidden. I could see out of an opening from the loft. Anyone who would be coming my way I would see.

After a few minutes I had an idea that I thought could work I went back down the stairs and found a piece of rope in the tackle room. I fastened a hangman's noose from the rope and took it back up the stairs to the loft with me. I then settled down and waited.

At seven forty-five, the senator came from around his house riding his golf cart, headed straight for the stables. Perfect, he was alone, when he arrived at the stables he came inside. I could hear him downstairs talking to his horses. I then left my hiding place. With my backpack in my left hand and my pistol in my right hand I crept down the stairs. When the senator spotted me I was less than thirty feet from him. He had a look of surprise, of shock, and disbelief on his face. At the same time I sensed that he knew this might be coming.

He just simply said, "Oh my god, no." I told him, "Approach me." He didn't say anything. I stopped him at the landing leading up to the loft. I opened my backpack and pulled the rope out. I then pulled his file out and laid it before him. I told the Senator, "I need you to look in the file and look carefully."

The senator took the file and carefully studied the information that I had laid before him. When the Senator was finished he laid the file down and said, "There is only one way you could have this much information about my life. It was provided to you by the government, the CIA, FBI, maybe even possibly the NSA. If you were sent here to kill me then I would already be dead, so exactly what do you want?" I said, "Senator you are right about how the information came to be in my possession, but what you are wrong about is whether or not you should be dead already. Senator you are going to die here today but I will give you an opportunity to save your wife, children, and grandchildren."

The senator became emotional at this point. He was telling me that his family has nothing to do with any of this. I told him that I agreed and that is why I was going to give him a chance to save them. The senator told me, "Explain yourself."

I told the senator, "The powers at be preferred his death be a suicide or an accident. I want you to hang yourself. If you do not I will shoot you in the head, go up to his house, shoot your wife, and anyone else who was there. I would then come back put the gun in your hand, making it a murder suicide. After that I will find your children and grandchildren, killing all of them as well. I have the rope here and I have a gun, it is your choice."

The senator then offered me a bribe, "Let me go and you can take the money I have in my house in a safe. I will just disappear. You can say that you didn't have the opportunity to kill me." I then told the senator, "Lay flat on the floor." I tossed the rope over a rafter. While standing on the landing I pulled the other end back and tied it off. I told the senator, "Get up and come up here on the landing."

When he walked to the landing I told him, "Put the rope around your neck or I will shoot you." He reluctantly put the rope around his neck, all the while trying to talk me out of killing him. As he was pleading his case I stepped forward and pushed him off the landing. The senator was swinging in mid air about two feet off the ground and was grabbing at the rope, trying to hold himself up. I walked over to where he was hanging and grabbed his legs in a bear hug. I lifted him up and with my full body weight I jerked him down, snapping his neck. I then picked up his file and checked to make sure I had not disturbed anything.

I did not dare leave the stable during daylight hours since there was no cover to hide myself. At this point I went back up stairs to the hay loft and settled into the pocket I had created.

A little before eleven o'clock the hired hand pulled up in his pick-up truck. He discovered the senator and immediately within twenty minutes the police and an ambulance were on the scene. Within two hours the stable was full of police, FBI, CIA, medical examiners, his wife crying in the background, and someone must have tipped the media. They were there trying to get the scoop from the outside. Helicopters were flying overhead, all the while I was up stairs just a few feet from everyone and more than once that day someone came up stairs to the loft and looked around. Finally, they removed the body and people began to leave. That night under the cover of darkness I hiked back to my cabin on Kentucky Lake. I showered and turned in for the night.

The next day I was heading back to Chicago. Upon arriving in Chicago I met up with Nick. Things were still fine.

After that I contacted Mike Walters. He was very pleased with the work I had just completed. Mike gave me the address of the Marine I was looking for. Mike still stood on his belief that I should let it go, but gave me the address anyway and said, "Go, get it over with or leave it be."

The marine I was looking for lived in Davenport, IA. His name was Nathan Daniels. He was married and had three children. I decided that I would take care of this business right away. I talked to Nick all of the orders for the product have been handled for the month. There was no reason I could not slip away. Nick did tell me, "Steven Besteto, of the Giania family, made a comment about the fact that you disappear from time to time." He said that it made him nervous not knowing where I was or what I was doing.

Three days later I headed for Davenport, IA. When I arrived in Davenport I rented myself a hotel room. The next day I drove by Nathan Daniels house. He lived in your typical middle class neighborhood. It appeared to me that no one was home so I came back that evening. This time I parked down the street where I could still see his house. Just before sunset he walked out of the house and went into a detached garage located on the back of his property.

I exited my car and walked into his garage where he was working on a late model Chevy. He asked me, "Can I help you?" I told him, "You most certainly can." As I pulled my pistol with a silencer, Nathan asked, "Do I know you? Have I done something to you to make you come to my house and point a pistol at me? Are you sure you have the right person?" I told Nathan, "I am absolutely sure I have the right person .If you are going to help torture somebody and help to pull six of their fingernails out you, should at least remember what they look like." Nathan then said, "It's you. You're the one from Vietnam."

"That's right," I told him. I then placed three shots into his chest and one to the head.

Before leaving I took his scalp and ears. I put both of them into a small sandwich bag and placed the bag into my coat pocket. I spent the night in my hotel and then headed back to Chicago.

I arrived in Chicago that afternoon and went straight to B & B's gentlemen club to see how things were doing. Business was good, the customers were spending their money, and the girls were looking great. I went back to my manager's office with Tim Hopkins to go over the books.

We were in the office for maybe an hour when one of the girls knocked on the door, it was Tina. She came to tell me that there were two men out front asking for me. I turned to look through the two way mirror, I had Tina point out the two men and just as soon as she did I recognized them both. They were two of Albert Giania's men. I thanked Tina and gave her a pat on her ass. She giggled, then left the room. She was not very bright, but for obvious reasons was one of my favorites.

I called up to the front and told the bartender, "Fix those men a drink on the house and tell them that I will be out to see them in a few minutes." I finished my business with Tim before going to the bar to see what they wanted. When I approached them they told me, "Albert wants to see you right away. You should come with us."

I am paranoid by nature and was not too eager to take a ride with them. I told them, "I will call Albert and set up a meeting." They insisted, "You will come with us right now." The one even pulled his jacket back, so that I could see his pistol. I told him, "Give me a break." I then pulled my jacket back to show him my pistol. I told the both of them, "We can have a good old fashion shoot out right here or you can just have Albert call me."

Ten minutes later Albert called. I asked him, "Is there a problem?" Albert said, "That is what I want to find out." Well neither one of us was going to talk too much on the phone. So I agreed to come to him. I told his two men, "That I would follow them to where ever Albert was, but in my own car."

We ended up in the back room of the night club "The Blue Velvet", it was owned by Besteto. When I walked into the back room I saw Nick sitting on the couch and then I had one of Albert's men relieve me of my weapons. I approached Albert; he was sitting at a table with Steve Besteto.

Albert said, "Have a seat." He then asked me, "Is there something you want to tell me?" I told him, "It is your party. Is there something you want to ask me?" Albert asked me, "Where have you been?" I told him, "I was out of town on personal business." Albert expressed to me, "You seem to be out of town on personal business quite often and that makes me nervous."

I told him, "If I told you what my personal business was then it would not be personal business anymore, now would it?" Albert barked back, "Cavanaro, there are people who believe that either yourself or your boy Nick are working with the Fed's. Now you need to tell me, where have you been?" "Albert, by people, do you mean that piece of shit over there Steven." Steven spoke up, "That's right. I do not trust you." I told Steven, "Trust has nothing to do with it. You simply just do not like me and the reason you did not like me is because I took care of your friend "Jingles". You are letting your dislike of me cloud your business decisions."

Steven claimed, "This is not the case." he claimed, "Your life is to secretive and you are hiding something." I then turned to Albert, "You are a man of great intelligence and reasoning. Albert, if it were not for that you would not be where you are at today. Steven simply dislikes me. I can appreciate this as well as sympathize with his feelings, but Albert you are smarter than that. Do not let him cloud your judgment. Do not let him cause you to make a decision that could cost money."

"Just tell me, where you have been? Help me understand, so that I can help Steven understand."

"Alright," I told Albert. I will tell you this one time and I will never tell you anything about my personal business again. If that is not enough for you then you can end it right now." Albert nodded his head and then told me, "Tell me, where you have been." If you can convince me that you are right and that Steven is wrong. Steven is yours to do as you please, but if you cannot convince me. Nick and you are Steven's to do as he pleases. Do you understand me?" I nodded and told Albert, "From time to time I go to Asia to keep the pipeline open. This allowed me to keep my contacts happy. This accounts for some of my disappearances'. There is also a woman that I have developed a relationship with after leaving Chicago in 1968. She lives out west. This accounts for most of, as you put it, my disappearances'. As far as to where I was most recently, I was settling an old score from Vietnam. I was assigned to a special project and I answered to no one on the base where I was stationed. The thought that an enlisted man did not have to answer to him, drove the general crazy. The thought that I came and went as I pleased was more than he could bear. So, one night I was visited by three military police. They tried to make me tell them what my assignment was, they worked on me for a long time, even pulled six of my fingernails out, but I never talked. Finally, they left me for dead." I was sure to let them know that I have killed the general and two of the military police and on my last trip was to Davenport, IA I killed the last remaining one. It took me a while to locate him, but I finally found him.

Before Albert could speak Steven started talking shit. Saying crap like, "Albert, he is making this shit up as he goes. He is a fucking liar and he knows that he is busted. I do not believe one fucking word of what he just said."

Albert then expressed to me, "Maybe what you said was true, but you did not convince me. Like Steven said, anyone can give a story, but to prove yourself is a whole different ball game."

At this point things were not looking good for me as well as Nick. Suddenly, I remembered the sandwich bag that I had put in my jacket pocket. The one, in which contained the scalp and ears. I told Albert, "If you will allow me to retrieve something out of my coat pocket I can prove beyond a reasonable doubt that everything I told you is true."

Albert called one of his men over to the table and told him, "If either of these two make a wrong move, shoot them." He then told me, "Retrieve whatever you have in my coat pocket, but be *very* careful about it."

All eyes were on me, you could have heard a pin drop it was so quiet. With my right hand I slowly reached into my jacket pocket and pulled the sandwich bag out. I laid it before Albert. He leaned back with a look of puzzlement on his face. He looked at me, then at the sandwich bag, and then to me again saying, "Is that what I think it is?" I told Albert, "What you are looking at is the scalp and the ears of the last one of the men that tortured me."

Albert wanted to know, "Why the fuck would you take a man's scalp and ears? That is some fucking sick shit. I have always known that you were not right in the fucking head, but God-damn, his scalp and ears."

I told Albert, "Old habits are hard to break. Taking a trophy after a kill was a habit I picked up in Vietnam and if you were not there, you wouldn't understand. The bottom line is that I have proven what I said was true." Albert agreed that he couldn't argue with that. Albert then said, "As a man of honor, a man of his word, and as much as it pains me Steven is yours to do with as you please."

The look on Stevens face was *priceless*. He just sat there, speechless. Albert got up from the table, looked at Steven, and told him, "I am sorry, but business is business and you have created a problem because of your personal feelings towards Cavanaro." Albert then excused himself from the room. I stood up and told Albert's men, If Steven moves, shoot him." I walked over to talk to Nick to make sure he was ok. This time no one touched him, he was unharmed.

I then told Albert's other men, "Give me back my pistol." I walked up to where Steven was sitting and told him, "I guess we are going to end this problem here and now." Steven just stared at me, he said nothing. He was prepared for what was about to happen or at least he thought he was.

I laid my pistol on the table in front of him and extended my hand in friendship. Steven looked at me and said, "I don't understand. Are you not going to kill me?" I told him, "It would not bother me, but I am not going to kill you, and *only* because I could tell that Albert really did not want it. I understand your dislike of me because I killed your longtime friend "Johnny Jingles," but if I had not, Johnny would have eventually killed me." Steven knew this to be true. He could not argue that point.

I let him know that we are at a crossroad, you can take my hand in friendship and let the past stay where it belongs. Allowing us to move on to the future and try to establish a better relationship with each other. Your other option is to take a bullet. I told him it was his call. It took very little thought on Steven's part before he took my hand in friendship. Now whether or not he meant it was another thing. Whether I will regret the decision to let him live, only time would tell.

I picked up the sandwich bag off the table and put it back into my coat pocket. I walked over to Nick and told him, "Come on. It is time for us to go." Nick stood up and then told me, "First, there is something I need to take care of." He walked over to Steven and hit him in the face with an overhand right, so hard his feet left the ground. Nick then stood over him and said, "I do not appreciate being called a snitch or being forced at gun point to this bullshit meeting. If you fuck with me again, I will *personally* kill you." Nick then extended his hand to help Steven up off the floor. He looked at him and said, "No hard feelings, but you had that coming." Steven just nodded.

After we left and were in the car driving back to B & B's Gentlemen's Club I asked Nick, "Where did that come from, you hitting Steven like that?" Nick told me, "It's like you always say we cannot afford to appear as if we are weak." I just smiled and shook my head.

We went back to the club and had a grand old time that night. There is something about being in a room full of naked women and knowing that you can have anyone of them or as many as you want, makes it hard to be anything, but in a good mood.

I went by Tony's car dealership the next day and we talked about a variety of things. Tony was especially impressed with the fact that I allowed Steve to live, even though I had Albert's permission to do as I pleased. Tony felt that Steven would calm down after the way things turned out and that would be better for everybody. Tony said he hoped that I had finally come to the realization that solving a problem without bloodshed was always the best option. It is better for business.

I asked Tony, "Are you and Albert happy with the way things were going in regards to the product?" Tony said that both he and Albert are very pleased. Like you, our biggest problem has become how we move, how to hide, and what to do with that much money. We both agreed these were problems we could live with.

CHAPTER TWENTY

September, 1975, the second B & B's Gentlemen club was ready to open. They were still working on the apartment building and the tunnel was almost complete. All that was left was to make the connection to the corner apartment.

After the apartment building itself was completed I invited Cathy Finch to the grand opening of club number two. She told me, "I appreciate the invitation, but I will have to decline the offer."

The opening was a success. The place was packed, the customers were spending, the girls were looking great, and fun was being had by all. I was sitting in a corner booth with Nick surrounded by naked women when I looked up to see Cathy Finch standing in front of me. Cathy said, "I had just stopped by to see the club. I did not mean to impose on your good time. I will be leaving." I jumped up to ask her, "Will you stay?" Cathy told me, "You seem to have your hands full already."

I turned to Nick and the girls and asked them, "Please move your party to another table. I am entertaining an important guest." We sat down and I ordered us a drink. I asked Cathy, "What is the real reason you are here tonight?" Cathy told me she had never been in this type of club and her curiosity brought her here.

We talked for several hours and finally, I went for the gold. I asked her, "Do you want to see the upstairs apartment?" Cathy told me, "You could have your pick of any woman in the club. You do not need me to go up to your apartment."

I told Cathy, "You are correct, I could have any woman in either one of my clubs if I chose to, but tonight I only wanted to spend time with you." Cathy laughed out loud. She told me, "I appreciate the effort and that was a pretty good pick up line but I'm afraid I cannot accept your offer."

We quickly moved on. I was a little too embarrassed to keep begging. A little later Cathy said, "I should be going." I may have been embarrassed, but I am not too proud that I would not try again. I asked her, "Are you sure you do not want to see the upstairs apartment and possibly have breakfast with me?" Cathy smiled and said, "You do not give up easily do you?" I told her, "I have never quit on anything in my life, especially something I really want."

Cathy turned and walked away, but stopped only after a few feet and came back to where I was standing and asked, "If I were to go to your apartment and have breakfast with you, would you call me tomorrow?" I told her, "No, I probably would not. I am not looking for a long term relationship." Cathy said, "In that case, why don't you show me your apartment?" I wasted no time taking her from the club up to the apartment.

We took a quick tour of the apartment. She like the office, I had it set up with all the video cameras. We watched the video screens for awhile then we ended up in the bedroom. She was everything I thought she would be and then some. The next morning we woke up, cleaned ourselves up, and then went to a nice restaurant for breakfast.

I told Cathy that I had to ask her. She said that I looked serious. "What is your question?" she asked. My question to you is, "Why is it that women like yourself, a women who is extremely attractive, very intelligent, and no doubt a women of class, show up in the club and agree to spend the evening with me? Do not take this the wrong way, I am very grateful for the evening, but in no way am I serious about a relationship. I am just curious." Cathy told me, "I also am not serious about a relationship and I also wondered why I spent the evening with you. I can only attribute it to me never in my life have been with a *bad boy.*" She was attracted to the fact that I was at least in her mind, a *bad boy.*

We both agreed we did not want a relationship though we might get together from time to time.

After breakfast she went her way and I went mine. Later that day I had the florist deliver to her office twelve dozen roses with a card that said only, "Wow!"

Towards the end of September, Nick and I went to Los Angeles to extend the pipeline. We met with a man named Allen Brown. It was the same set up as always in a health club, in the sauna, taking a steam and sealing the deal. Allen Brown was there to represent the Balanco family. This family had established themselves in Los Angeles in the late 1950's. He tried to argue about the price, but I told him I would not wavier on my prices. After some slightly heated debate he finally agreed to pay what I was asking. His first order, like most, was five kilos of product. The method of delivery and payment would be the same as always. After the deal was closed Nick and I stayed in Los Angeles for two more days setting things up. We were making sure that everything was in place.

Nick had commented to me, "I would have never thought we could have possibly established connections in nine different major cities to move the product in just one year." I told Nick, "That is because we priced the product lower than anyone else could provide it for. The product was basically selling itself. Nick then told me, "The FBI has just over thirty agents working full time collecting information thru wire taps and video surveillance, so that they can build a case against the large number of people in the connected cities." The places we were moving the product to and the number of people involved was growing every day. This along with the number of agents who are tracking the people involved. This would without a doubt be the single largest investigation the FBI has ever been involved with.

Nick seemed proud of what we were doing I unfortunately did not share these same feelings. I was doing it for the money and maybe even more for the adrenaline rush. When we were ready to fly back and leave Los Angeles I told Nick, "I will be staying behind for a week or so, I will call you." Nick knew by now not to ask me what I was doing or where I was going. He just said, "That's fine, just call me and let me know who is buying what and when the product will be there. I will take it from there." With that said he took a cab to the airport.

I slipped out of the hotel through the service entrance. I took a cab to a car rental place and headed out for Cider Falls. I was headed for Sarah. I drove through the night arriving at my lake house at four o'clock in the morning. I was too tired to contact Sarah that day, so instead I just rested.

That day I made use of the tunnel for the first time. The room to the tunnels entry, which I had built as part of the tunnel, would act as storage. I had put up some shelving along the walls. I had deposited two million dollars, in hundred dollar bills, on the shelves. They were bundled up into five hundred thousand dollar packages that were shrink-wrapped in plastic to keep them safe. Having money spread around the world in varies numbered accounts was a great thing, but having a good stash of hard cash was the best insurance policy anyone in the world could have. I saw no reason why I shouldn't keep adding to my cash collection in the future.

About this time I also started a collection of things like C-4 explosives. You never know when you might need a little help with a problem. An average person might not think that someone could buy C-4, hand grenades, a hand held bazookas, but you would be wrong. With enough money you can buy *anything* you want, all you have to do is know the right people, or the wrong ones. This all depends on your point of view. God bless America, and the capitalist who run it.

The next day when I woke up I called the lodge, Sarah's husband, Daniel, answered. I told Daniel, "I will be coming home in two days and I would appreciate if you could have Sarah clean the house for me before I arrive? Daniel told me, "I will be glad to give her the message and I will make sure that she takes care of it for you." When I hung the phone up I had to laugh, make sure she takes care of you. Daniel had no idea just how good his wife Sarah was taking care of me.

Later that day just before noon Sarah showed up. We immediately embraced each other. She started to cry and trembled. I asked her, "Sarah, what is wrong? Are you ok?" She replied, "Of course I am ok. If you loved me as much as I love you, you would be crying right now too."

"Sarah, I *do* love you as much as you love me, but I cannot cry. I have never been able to show my emotions in that way, but just because I cannot cry on the outside does not mean that I am not crying on the inside. You are the only part of my life that makes me happy. You are the only part of my life that makes sense to me. You are the only part of my life that I look forward to. You must know that by now, you have to know that by now."

Sarah looked me in the eye and then gave me a kiss. She told me, "As a woman I have the right to act this way and not to worry. I know how you feel about me." Sarah then took me by the hand and led me back to the bedroom.

We spent the rest of the afternoon with each other. We made love several times and when we weren't making love we held each other close. Neither one of us wanted to let the other one go. We treated every moment we had together as if though it might have been the last. Just writing about, Sarah, expressing how I feel about her, makes my heart race. I cannot fully explain it, but Sarah is the only part of my life that could be considered even close to normal.

Around four o'clock she had to leave. Sarah told me, "Tomorrow I will be back. I will tell Daniel that she needed to go grocery shopping for you, and that I needed to finish cleaning the house. We exchanged a kiss and a hug then she was gone. As good as I had felt for being with her that day, I was just as sad to see her go. It was around ten-thirty when she showed up at my house the next morning and we went straight to the bedroom for a session of love making. After an hour Sarah jumped out of bed, and told me, "We are not going to lie in bed all day. Instead, I am going to make us a nice lunch." She prepared a wonderful meal that we ate outside, in the boathouse, overlooking the lake. It was October and the weather was starting to feel crisp. I don't believe we could have asked for a nicer day. While there we ate, drank, and sat around talking for hours. Sarah told me, "I need to clean up from lunch and go back to the lodge." We both stood up, I turned and looked at Sarah with a big smile on my face I took my arm and cleared the contents of the table onto the floor. "There, the table has been cleared; does that buy me any extra time for some more extracurricular activities?" She laughed and said, "You are a *bad boy*."

I took Sarah into my arms and we then made love on the table in the boathouse. I believe we both found it to be a little dangerous and very exciting. Afterwards Sarah said, "Call the lodge tomorrow and thank me for my services." We both laughed at that comment then Sarah said, "I will invite you over for dinner with the family." We once again kissed then hugged and she left.

Now I was stuck with cleaning up the mess I had made. It seemed like a good idea at the time. Who am I kidding, it was a great idea!

The next day, as planned, I called the lodge to thank Sarah for her services. I started laughing and Sarah then mumbled under her breath, "You are so bad. Will you have dinner with my family?"

Later that evening I showed up at the lodge at five-thirty. Dinner was to be served at six o'clock. I decided to a have drink with her father before we ate dinner. He was a good man; I always liked both he and his wife. It was a few minutes to six when Sarah's mother came into the great room where we were having our drinks and informed us that dinner was ready.

When we came into their private dining room there sat Daniel and Sarah's son, Michael. He was getting big, almost five years old now. He looked more Italian than Indian, but at any rate I could see he had his mothers eyes when I looked at him. Michael was a well behaved and pleasant child. During dinner Daniel asked me, "Have you seen the new addition to the lodge?" I told him, "I have not noticed anything different." Daniel seemed very proud to tell me that they had added a horse stable and that they currently had four horses. Daniel said, "Training horses is a hobby of mine. One that Sarah does not share with me." One could easily tell by the look on Sarah's face that she could care less about the horses.

Sarah moved the conversation forward, no doubt to avoid more talk about the horses. She asked me, "Is your house in good order?" Was there anything that I may have over-looked? I told Sarah, "The house looked great and I am very pleased with your services." I pulled an envelope out of my jacket pocket and handed it to Sarah." This should cover what you spent on groceries and payment for cleaning the house. I appreciate it very much." Sarah smiled then thanked me.

It was then that saw Daniel reached over and took the envelope with the money that I had intended for Sarah. Daniel folded it in half and then tucked it into his back pocket. Sarah at this point would not look at me, but Daniel on the other hand looked at me and smiled. He continued to eat his dinner as if though taking the money that I had intended for Sarah was ok. I did understand that they were married and that a man should be in control of the family and its finances, but what Daniel did not know is that the thought of him being married to Sarah sickened me. The thought of him putting his hands on her body *enraged* me.

I actually opened the wrist watch, the one given to me by Mike Walters, so that I could see the cyanide capsules hidden inside. For a moment I considered putting one in his drink, but then thought better of the idea. Not that I was opposed to killing Daniel, but not like that, not now. So for the time being Daniel would be safe. That is for the time being because I am not sure just how long I can resist the urge to make him go away.

I spent the next few days resting. I told Sarah, "I will be leaving and you should tell Daniel that you need to go to my house tomorrow to straighten up and put the house back in order."

As planned, the next day Sarah came by early in the morning. Sarah said that she couldn't be gone more than a few hours. She did not waste any time getting to the bedroom.

Before Sarah left I asked her, "Why did you give Daniel the money that was intended for you?" Sarah told me, "It is just the way things worked. Daniel controlled the money and it is the same with my parents, it is expected of me." I handed Sarah five hundred dollars and told her, go spend it on yourself. Sarah handed it back to me and said, "If I spent money on myself, Daniel will find out." I told Sarah, "Take the money, hide it, and maybe someday you can use it when you really needed it." We said our goodbyes and I told Sarah, "I will try to be back to see you by spring."

A few days later I was back in Chicago and the next few weeks went by fast. Before I knew it there was only ten days left till Christmas. I spent most of my time at the club, after all I lived upstairs. All of the girls at the club were wearing Santa hats, g-strings, and nothing else. I decided to shut the club down on Christmas day only. Some of the girls had no family and no place to go, I also had no place to go. Nick told me he also had no place to go, so we decided to throw a party. It would be at my main club and it was for anyone who had nothing else to do or no one to be with. It turned out to be Nick, myself and thirteen very attractive young ladies. A good time was had by all and the next day we reopened business as usual.

CHAPTER TWENTY-ONE

It was time to get ready for the big New Years Eve parties at the clubs. I invited Cathy to the party, but she declined. She had already made plans. I lost interest in the parties. It was then and there that I decided, right or wrong; I will go home to see my mother.

It was risky so I had to be careful. I slipped out of town under the cover of darkness and drove through the night. The next morning, about one hour from my mother's farm, I checked into a hotel. I spent that day and night at the hotel preparing myself. The next morning I awoke early and headed for my mother's house I have been known for having nerves of steel, but that morning my stomach was tied up in knots. The hour drive to the farm seemed to last forever.

When I arrived at the driveway to the farm house I pulled in and stopped. I was not sure even at this point whether or not I could go ahead with my plans. I sat for three or four minutes before proceeding to the house. When I pulled up it was nine o'clock in the morning. Before I could knock on the door my mother ran out of the house to greet me. She was wearing a familiar cotton dress, an apron, and a pair of house slippers. She was nuts for running through six inches of snow as if it were not there. She ran up to me crying hysterically. I grabbed her; she was sobbing, out of breath, and became weak as if though she might faint. I scooped her up and carried her into the house placing her on the sofa. After I gave her a glass of water and after a few minutes went by she could talk without crying. We talked for almost an hour. She then went to the back porch and rang the bell. Its primary use was to let you know when it was time to eat, but it also served as an emergency bell. When she rang that bell my brothers, Terry and Todd, came out of the equipment shed where they had been working. They wasted no time getting to the house to see what mother needed. When they came in the back door thru the kitchen they both just froze when they saw me.

Finally, Todd extended his hand then pulled me in tight. He patted me on the back and said, "It is good to see you brother." Terry did likewise. My mother decided she would start calling people to tell them I have come home. I had to stop her and tell her, "You can only call Debbie if you want to, but no one else." She didn't understand.

She wanted to tell the world her son had finally came home. I told her, "When Debbie shows up I will explain everything to everyone, but for now you have to trust me." My mother reluctantly agreed. She then decided she would prepare a feast for the family. I suppose in her mind it was a celebration of some sort.

While mother was busy in the kitchen I went outside with my brothers to help them with their chores. They both started to ask questions that I did not want to answer at that time. I told them both, "When Debbie gets here I will explain everything to everyone at one time. I just do not want to repeat myself all day." They both understood. We were outside for a few hours tending to the livestock and working on one of the tractors.

They both made fun of the fact that my hands were soft. My hands were no longer those of a farmer. They were right, the calluses' I once had were gone. I do know that in those few hours outside with my brothers, it was if though I had gone back in time and the last ten years never happened. I almost expected to see my father come around the corner at any moment. It was very peaceful then suddenly as to have been awakened from a dream; the bell rang out once more that day.

It meant only one thing. My sister Debbie was now here. The three of us went back to the house and upon entering the house I was greeted by Debbie. She was tearful and happy to see me. I asked her, "Where are your husband and your son?" Debbie said, "They stayed home. I was not sure if they should come." I told Debbie, "I would have liked to of seen them. Debbie said, "There is always tomorrow." Debbie and mother worked in the kitchen while we boys visited.

Later that day we had a wonderful meal; the kind of meal that only your mother could prepare. This brings back childhood memories. After dinner with all of us sitting at the dining room table I began to tell them where I have been and what I have been doing for the last ten years. I told them as much as I could. I told them, "After leaving the farm I ended up in California doing odd jobs. After talking to Debbie and finding out about Craig dying in Vietnam, I joined the Marines. Spent time in Vietnam and during my time in the Marines I became involved in a special assignment that eventually led me to do work for the government after I was discharged from the Marines.

I told them, "What I am telling you, though I know it is vague, is all I can tell you about my life. None of you can tell anyone that you have had contact with me because of the nature of what I do. There are people out there that would use you to get to me and at this point I was not sure that coming back to see you is not a mistake. My worst fear would be that something might happen to you all because I made an appearance in your lives."

I made all of them promise not to talk about my visit. They agreed. I then told them, "I have brought a gift to be shared by everyone." After going to my car and retrieving a suitcase I came back in and laid it on the dining room table. When I opened it they all starred at the contents not speaking.

The suitcase contained two million dollars in cash all in one hundred dollar bills; wrapped in ten thousand dollar packets. Finally, my sister said, "Is this for us?" "Yes, this is for the four of you. Don't ask me where it came from because if you knew, your life would be in danger. Just make sure you do not draw attention to yourself. Spend it slowly; a little here and there. Do not put it in the bank and do not make large purchases. This money will help you throughout your lives. Just be careful with how you handle it."

After that we talked for hours. Finally, my sister headed home and my brothers turned in for the night. Mother and I sat up until 2a.m. talking that night. When I went to bed, I stayed in the room I had as a child. It was *exactly* as I had left it.

The next morning when I awoke I realized that it was probably a mistake to come back. No matter how much I wanted it, my life was so far removed from the life I once had on the farm. Being here is going to make it harder on everyone, including me. It may have been better if I had just remained missing.

I told my mother, "I need to go to town to make a phone call I cannot use your phone and I will be back soon." My mother started crying and she made me promise I would be back. Somehow she knew I left her a letter on my bed.

When I left it was one of the hardest things I have ever had to do, but it was the best thing for everyone involved. Satisfying my own urge to see my family could very well place them in danger and I will not allow that to happen. It was a mistake I would not repeat again.

I returned to Chicago and got back to business as usual. This was my life, not being on the farm I grew up on, but instead the life I had made for myself. No matter how fucked up it was, it was mine.

March of 1976, I contacted Cathy Finch, my favorite real estate agent to see about buying some more properties. I wanted to expand on the B & B's Gentlemen's club franchise. By June we had settled on two properties and my contractor told me they would both be open by October. I thought this would be a good time to ask Cathy to celebrate. To my surprise Cathy agreed.

We spent a very enjoyable weekend together in Atlantic City and as promised both the new clubs were opened by October. I was able to talk Cathy into coming to both grand openings for the new clubs and as a bonus Cathy went back to the main club where I had my living quarters to spend a night of pure enjoyment with me. Cathy was definitely not Sarah, but she was a reasonably good substitute.

I was on top of the world, I had four clubs, a townhouse, an apartment, the apartment building behind my main club was open, the tunnel was complete, and I could come and go as I pleased. I had the lake house in Cider Falls and I could have a different woman every night if I wanted to. Not to mention Nick and I are now moving over five hundred kilos of product per month. The money was coming in non-stop.

November of 1976, Cathy and I began looking for a piece of land where I could build a house. I turned down multiple locations and then finally, I saw the right piece of land. There was on older home on one hundred eighty acres of land and it was only an hour drive to Chicago. The property even had road frontage on two sides. I only wanted to buy the land. The owner said, "If someone else will buy the house and ten acres I will be willing to split the property."

The next day, through a different real estate agent under a false identity, I bought the house and ten acres. I then bought the remaining one hundred and seventy acres under the name of David Cavonaro. I contacted my old contractor, the same one who built the lake house and renovated the properties for me in Chicago, and this time I wanted my new house built on the land I had just purchased.

It was to be built within two thousand feet of the old farm house. The two were to be connected by a tunnel. The tunnel will come out under the garage of the old farm house. In the new house it could be accessed from the master bedroom on the second floor, the den on the first floor, and from the basement. The basement was a walk out, this way I was able to put an electric golf cart in the tunnel and could turn around in the twelve foot by twelve foot room on either end.

I spent nearly nine million dollars on the tunnel alone, but my own paranoia is what I believe keept me alive. Besides it is just money and like I said, "It just keeps coming in." The work began in the spring of 1977 and it would take until the summer of 1978 to complete. This was fine, in the mean time I had plenty to do.

I have not seen Sarah in over one year. It was time for a road trip. I went through the tunnel from my living quarters at the club over to the corner apartment. Before leaving I changed clothes, put on a long wig with a pony tail, some glasses, a beard, and a ball cap. When I left the apartment I would be someone else.

I kept a car parked in the parking lot set up for the tenants of the apartment building. This way I am free to come and go as I please. No one was ever able to figure out how I came and went without being detected. I know this was something that irritated everyone because from time to time Mike Walters would tell me, "Eventually I will figure out how you manage to become invisible." I would always just look at him and smile.

When I arrived in Cider Falls the same tactics were employed as always. I was eagerly waiting for Sarah to show up at the lake house. When she finally arrived we embraced, but something was wrong. Something was different, I could sense it. "Sarah, are you ok?" I asked, "Is everything alright?"

Sarah looked at me in the eyes and broke down crying. "No, everything is not ok."

"My parents were killed in a car accident; they were hit by a logging truck head on. They died instantly." I do not believe it was much comfort to Sarah to know her parents had died instantly. Her parents have only been gone for three weeks. I apologized to Sarah for having not been available to talk to her about what she had gone through. Sarah was emotional and made a commit to me about being so secretive about my life and how she hated that. There was nothing I could do nothing to change what had already been done. I could only be there to listen, to support, and to understand what Sarah was feeling. Though the offer was made, there would be no love making on this trip home. I wanted to be with her badly, but it just felt wrong, after all Sarah did mean much more to me then someone whom I could have sex with.

Sarah and I went to the cemetery the next day to visit the graves of her parents. I always liked both her mother and her father. They would be missed by all.

I stayed for nine days on that trip. Sarah and I spent as much time together as her schedule would allow. In the end, Sarah was not angry at me. She knew that our relationship, for better or worse, was what it was and that wishful thinking at least for now would not change anything. When I left to return to Chicago, I was feeling somewhat down. It was nice to see Sarah, but it was not a very pleasant trip. I returned to Chicago and went back to what I normally did.

In April, Mike Walters contacted me to take care of a problem. It appeared that a gentleman whom they have been looking for a number of years has been located. His name was Gerald Brown. He was living in New Zealand under an assumed name. He now went by the name Larry Gregson.

When I arrived in New Zealand, it was under a false identity and I would play the role of a tourist. As always, I spent several days tracking my target and taking in the sights. On the evenings of the fourth day I let myself into his home. I knew he was not there, but I also knew that he would eventually come home. Mike did not care how it was done, he just wanted it done. When he finally came home, I stayed hidden, in a closet, in the guest bedroom.

Within a few minutes I heard him running his bath water. I waited until he was taking his bath, making him an easy target. When I came into the bathroom he shouted, "Who are you? What do you want?" I told him, "I have been sent to take care of a problem and that you, Gerald Brown, are the problem.

Before he could react I pushed the radio he had plugged in on the sink top into the tub. The lights flickered while Mr. Gerald Brown thrashed about violently. It only lasted for a few seconds and it was over. The problem had been taken care of.

I then left as I had came, making sure to leave no trace of having ever been there. This type of work was easy. It was cut and dry, there was nothing difficult about it.

Two days later I would be back in Chicago and everything was going as planned. The product was flowing, as well as the cash. I spent almost all of my time at the clubs.

CHAPTER TWENTY-TWO

In June of 1977, Cathy Finch, whom I had not heard from in months, called for no reason. Cathy wanted to come by the club to see me. I had no problem with that. We spent the evening together, dining, dancing having drinks, and then we ended up back at the main club where Cathy spent the night with me. It was wonderful as always, the next morning Cathy was up early preparing to leave I asked her, "What is the hurry?" It was then that Cathy told me, "I am getting married and moving away. We cannot see each other again."

For a moment I did not know exactly what to say, so I simply said, "Congratulations. When is the big day?" Cathy told me, "I am getting married today and that is why I am up so early." I asked her, "If you are getting married why contact me and then stay the night?" Cathy said, "I knew it was the last time that I would ever do anything like this again and I just needed to get it out of my system."

I could only smile at that answer and then I asked her, "Do you have time to cleanse your system once more?" Cathy smiled, shook her head, quickly undressed, and jumped into bed with me. Thirty minutes later she was leaving. I never saw or heard from her again, I will miss her. Like I said before, "She is no Sarah, but she was a reasonably good substitute."

The work on my new house with the new tunnel system was now underway. It will be a year before completion, but that would be ok. There is no real hurry.

It was now September, 1977, and I recently found out that one of my top girls, Tina, who happened to be one of my favorites, was involved in a relationship with a man who was physically abusive to her. When I found this out those old feelings came rushing back. I knew as soon as I heard about the abuse toward Tina that I would be paying her gentlemen friend a visit, one he would never forget if he was fortunate enough to live through the visit. It took me a few days to find out what I needed to know about him. I had to find out his name, address, and where he worked. Once I had that information I would be able to carry out whatever plan I came up with. After following Tina's gentlemen friend, Bill Thornton, for a few days I decided that I would have to take care of this particular problem somewhere other than his home, since he was now living with Tina.

Bill Thornton was an iron worker to be exact; he at least on the surface was a loud person. He was one who gave the impression of being a tough guy. I knew where he was working and when he left work I followed him to a local bar. When he pulled in to the parking lot I pulled in right next to him. Before he could get out of his car I pointed a pistol at him and told him, "Drive."

He of course was understandably shaken and very nervous. "Who are you? What do you want?" I told Mr. Thornton, "Remain calm and do what I ask. Everything will be explained to you in due time." I had him drive to a vacant building a few blocks from the main club that I owned. I took him inside to the basement of the building. By now this tough guy was all, but crying. I tied him to a post and I gagged him. After that I left and made my way back to retrieve my car. After retrieving my car I stopped by the club to check in on a few things. I became preoccupied and almost forgot that Mr. Tough guy was tied to a post a few blocks away. Around two a.m. I went back to check on him. He was still there and he was looking like anything except a tough guy.

While in the basement I noticed a few rats. This gave me an idea, I hit Bill in the head with the butt of my pistol and while he was unconscious I retied him on his back, spread eagle, on the floor, and his mouth was gagged. He could not move nor could he cry out for help. When he came too I told him, "I hate men such as you, one who beats on women. You pretend to be tough when in reality you are cowards because only a coward would beat on woman." I then told him, "I was going to kill you out right, but I have changed my mind. Instead, I am going to leave you here for the rats and over the next few days they will slowly eat away at you until you are dead. They will continue to eat away at you until there is nothing left." I got up from my chair and left, leaving Mr. Bill Thornton there for the rats.

I returned days later to see what progress had been made. After three days the rats had eaten away him until I suppose they hit a major blood vessel and he must have bled to death or died from shock. Either way to me it was just one more cowardly prick who would never lay his hands on a woman again. I knew that Tina would be better off without him.

It was now November, 1977, and nothing unusual was happening. Things were just the opposite, the product was moving fine. Nick and I were up to seven hundred kilos per month and at five thousand dollars per kilo we were bringing in around fifteen million dollars a month. My share of that, after the CIA was reimbursed for their expenses, was over four million a month. I had more money than I could spend. I had all the women I wanted, but yet I was empty. I was not satisfied; I had become bored so it was time to make a trip to Cider Falls. I let Nick know that I would be gone for awhile.

As always I left through the tunnel from the club to the apartment. I decided to drive to Cider Falls so I put eighteen million dollars in the trunk of my car. The money had been stored in the tunnel leading from the club to the apartment.

When I arrived in Cider Falls I called Sarah to come over to clean. At least that is what Daniel always thought. Before Sarah arrived I deposited the eighteen million dollars in the tunnel at my lake house. I now had twenty three million dollars in the tunnel as well as another twenty million scattered around the world in numbered accounts.

Sarah finally arrived at the lake house. We spent the better part of the three hours making love, talking, and just catching up. The next day I went by the lodge for dinner. I ate my meal with Sarah's husband Daniel and their son Michael. Michael was six years old now and getting bigger every time I saw him. Sarah also ate dinner with us. It was a good meal and good conversation. By now Daniel considered me to be just an old family friend. Two days later Sarah came by to see me. She told me, "Daniel took a business trip to California to see a man about buying a new boats for the lodge."

We had to whole day to spend together. We ended up as we always did, in each other arms. Later that day when our hormones finally settled down Sarah confided in me, "Daniel and I are not getting along and we have discussed getting a divorce. The problem was that if I left he told me that he would take half the value of the lodge." This was a business that Sarah's parents had spent forty years of their life building. If she went through with it she would lose the lodge and she could not let that happen, so she would stay.

I asked Sarah, "Tell me why, were you two suddenly not getting along?" Sarah said, "Since my parent's death, Daniel is drinking more and more. Something he would not have done while my father was living. When he drinks he becomes mean." I immediately asked, "Does he hit you?" Sarah said, "So far he has never hit, it is just that when Daniel is drinking he tends to become loud and says terrible thing to both Michael and myself. Once or twice I thought he was going to hit me, but he never has."

This is all the information I needed. With the way I felt about Sarah and the way I feel about men who abuse women, I knew that Daniel had to go. He had to be taken care of. I knew that his death had to look like an accident; there is no question about that. I spent the next week studying Daniel, studying his habits, racking my brain trying to find a solution to this problem. One day, while at the lodge, Daniel asked me, "Do you want to go to the stables with me to feed the horses?"

Daniel seemed to feed his horses at five o'clock every night. While in the stables I asked Daniel, "Why is it that in front of every horse stable there is a wooden peg with horse shoes on it?" He claimed, "Horses, like people, wear different size shoes and that it is my way of storing the shoes until needed." Right then and right there I knew exactly how I would kill him. In my business sometimes when you least expect it, the perfect idea comes to you. For Daniel my inspiration was the horse shoes on the wooden peg.

The next day I informed Sarah that I will be leaving in the morning. Sarah was unable to get away to see me. Before I left I told Sarah, "I would try to call you in a few weeks."

The next morning I did not leave, instead I stayed. Later that afternoon I took a hike, making my way around the lake, towards the lodge. I was being very careful not to be spotted. When I approached the lodge I came up on the side of the lodge where the stables where located. I waited there for Daniel to feed his horses and like clockwork Daniel came into the stables at five o'clock.

As Daniel entered the stable I stepped out of the shadows and hit Daniel in the head with a baseball bat. Not just any baseball bat, but a baseball bat that I had attached a horseshoe to, a horseshoe I took earlier. When I struck him the horseshoe hit him square between the eyes leaving a horseshoe shaped mark on his head. I walked over to the stable from which I had removed the horseshoe from and let the appropriate horse loose, making it look as if though the horse kicked him in the head. This allowed me to make the entire thing look like an accident. I made my way back to the lake house in the early morning hours and I quietly left to head back to Chicago.

A few days later I was back in Chicago and before I left I had told Sarah, "I would call her in a few weeks." I waited three weeks before I called Sarah and when she answered the phone I could tell she was glad to hear from me. I could tell by the tone of her voice that something was wrong though. I asked, "Sarah is everything was ok?" It was then that Sarah told me, "Daniel was dead. He had been kicked in the head by one of the horses. He had died the day after you left."

I of course told her that I was so sorry to hear about her loss. I then asked Sarah, Is there anything I could do or if there was anything she needed? Sarah began to cry and told me, "She was not crying because Daniel was died, but because his death was actually a relief to her." Sarah said, "I am crying because my son, Michael, is so upset. Michael is taking the whole thing very hard."

There was not much I could say except, "Time will heal. As time passes, the pain will diminish until one day the pain becomes tolerable and Michael will be a strong young man." Sarah agreed, but knew that the following months would be difficult. I agreed and told her, "Though I might not be able to come back to Cider Falls with anymore frequency than I have in the past, I will make an effort to call more often."

I felt nothing from killing Daniel except joy and a sense of relief. After having spoken to Sarah I did feel badly for what she and her son Michael would have to go through, but in the end Sarah would be happier and that made me feel better. I kept my promise to Sarah, I did call her at least once a month if not more often than that.

CHAPTER TWENTY-THREE

It was now March, 1978, and my old friend Mike Walters had come by to get his monthly cut of the product. Mike and I did this once a month but yet there was something wrong. Not something a person could see, but something that a person could feel. It was then that I told Mike, "Whatever is on your mind, I wish you would just tell me." Mike looked at me then he cast his eyes down towards the floor. "God damn it Mike. How bad can it be? Just spill it. What do you require of me" Mike looked at me directly in the eyes and told me, "My wife is having an affair with a young man and it is tearing me up inside." I asked Mike; "Is your wife aware that you know about her affair?" He told me, "She is not aware. The reason I have not confronted her is because I myself, once had an affair. My wife is aware of it and maybe this was just something she needed to get out of her system. The problem is that she has been having the affair for almost a year and I feel that I might lose her. I was unsure of how to handle the situation to get the results I needed." The entire time Mike spoke I listened carefully, saying nothing. When he had finished I told him, "By confiding in me, you already determined how best to handle the situation. By confiding in me you can expect to get the same results that you got in Texas with your former son in law. There is no reason for either one of us to pretend. If you want this problem to go away, all you need to do is ask. Risk losing her, or ask." Mike drew a deep breath raised his head looked at me and said, "I am asking, will you make this problem go away?" I responded by telling Mike, "I have never denied you anything whether it were to be a business request or a personal favor. Taking care of this problem for you would be my pleasure." Mike told me, "I will pay for your services." I told Mike that I did not accept his offer of money and that instead I would take a rain check. Perhaps someday he could return the favor. He just nodded in agreement.

We then entered into a conversation pertaining to the information that I required in order to make Mike's problem go away. During the course of the conversation I found out that the gentlemen in question was Alexander Knoll. He is a thirty-eight year old Biology professor at West Virginia University, the same University that his wife taught, she was a Chemistry professor.

Mike also told me that Mr. Knoll had filed for a divorce just a few days ago. He felt as if it would not be long before his wife did the same. Mike asked, "Can you act quickly and discreetly?" It must seem as if it was an accident or from natural causes." I asked Mike, "Can you provide me with the same cocktails of chemicals that were provided to me while in Paris, France? This way it would appear to be a heart attack." He agreed.

The next day Mike and I met, he gave me the cocktail I asked for and soon after he left, I was on a plane for West Virginia.

It was two thirty when I arrived. A cab dropped me off at the University. When I arrived there I asked some student, "Where is Mr. Knoll's biology class located?"

It was easy enough to find. When I arrived at the classroom the students were just leaving. It was his last class of the day. As luck would have it when the last student exited the room I let myself in. I approached the desk and he asked, "Can I help you?"

At that point I took the hypodermic needle I had concealed and stuck it into his thigh. He jumped back and shouted, "What did you inject me with and why?"

I told Mr. Knoll, "You should not be sleeping with another man's wife." He had a look of utter disbelief on his face. He then suddenly grabbed his chest. The cocktail of chemicals was now running through his body. In just a few moments, after he grabbed his chest, Mr. Knoll was dead of a massive heart attack.

I exited the room and made my way back to the airport. I was back in Chicago by nine o'clock that evening. Mike Walters had what he wanted and maybe I earned a little credit. That little credit could be the difference between a good day and bad day.

The next time I saw Mike Walters I asked him, "Did things work out in your favor?" Mike told me, "My wife seemed to be slightly depressed for a few days and I can understand why. Her mood seemed to pass in a short period of time and for now things seemed to be ok."

In Mike's own words it was as if their relationship had renewed itself, Mike then thanked me and followed it up with, "I owe you for the two favors you have done for me. Someday, if possible, I will pay you back." Like I said, "A little credit cannot hurt."

The product was moving; sales were up from month to month. Everyone seemed happy at the moment, the gentlemen's clubs were booming and my new house would be ready in a few months. I had no particular reason to stay in town.

It was now May, 1978, I called Sarah quite often and I missed her more than ever. It was time for a road trip.

When I arrived, in Cider Falls I went to the lake. After dropping off some more money and a few personal affects at the lake house, I finally arrived at the lodge. Sarah was very excited to see me. I rented a room at the lodge and that night for the first time ever, after the day's work was done, Sarah came to my room and we were able to spend the entire night together. To see her for the first time in the early morning, with the sun bursting through the window, her hair was a mess, her makeup was in desperate need of attention, but to be able to see her just lying there, sleeping. Even now, is hard to describe in words. I cannot explain how I felt that first time. The only thing I can think of is I experienced over powering feelings of happiness. It was as if though my life before this moment did not exist.

Sarah finally woke up and asked me, "What are you looking at?" I just smiled and jumped out of bed, "Come on, lets' go, get up." She went back to her room to get ready. I later met her downstairs for breakfast. We spent the next eight days together before I headed back to Chicago.

When I arrived back to Chicago things were just as I had left them. It seems as though I have been given a nickname. The employees at my main club, where I was living, decided to start calling me, "The Ghost."

They claim they came up with the nickname, "The Ghost" because one minute I was there and the next minute I was gone. No one ever saw me come or go. I found the nickname to be humorous, if they only knew about the tunnel. I strongly suspect Nick had a hand in my new nickname because he has asked me more than once, "How the hell do you come and go without being detected?" I would always just smile saying nothing. Nick told me, "Someday, when this is all over, you have to tell me how the hell you do it." I would just smile and change the subject.

It was now July, 1978 and finally, my new house was done. The total cost for the new house, the tunnel, and the older house being connected to the tunnel, was just over seventeen million dollars. The majority of the cost was from the construction of the tunnel. It may seem like a great deal of money, but as I have stated in the past, "My own paranoia keeps me alive and if that tunnel saves my life, one time, or gives me the edge I need to take care of business then it was well worth every dollar."

Between July and August of 1978 I moved into my new home. I hired a company to care for the lawn, another to care for the pool, and I hired an older woman to take care of the house. Her name was Joan Lynch, she was allowed to work whatever hours she wanted as long as the house was clean, my laundry was done, and she prepared a meal for me on the rare occasion that I was home. I was ok with our arrangement.

Joan also lived at the house with me. She never commented on the strange hours I kept nor did she comment on the variety of women whom she saw come and go on a regular basis. Joan did her job and left me alone. In return I left Joan alone. It was almost like having your mom living with you, but not involving herself in your life. There were times when I would not see her for days, but I always knew that Joan was around the house was clean and there was always some sort of fresh baked goodies on the kitchen counter.

    Things were going so smooth that it made me nervous. Experience has taught me that trouble is very easy to come by. It seemed that my own paranoid nature would prove to be correct once again.

CHAPTER TWENTY-FOUR

Trouble was not only just around the corner, it was upon me before I knew it. I remember the exact date and time. It was 6:45pm on November 3rd, 1978. I remember it all too well. My phone rang, it was Nick. He was calling me from his place, he was in a panic, "I have been shot and he took the money. *He took the god damn money!*" "Are you ok Nick? Do you need medical attention?"

Nick then replied, "Do not worry about me, I am fine. You don't understand what I am saying, he took the money." I told Nick, "Stay where you are, do not call anyone. I will be there as quick as I can."

When I arrived at Nick's place he was still in a panic. The first thing I asked, "Nick, you said you where shot, are you ok?"

Nick lifted his shirt to reveal three spots on his chest where his bullet proof vest stopped the bullets, but definitely left three nasty marks on his chest. Once I realized that Nick was ok I then asked him, "Tell me exactly what happened." Nick said, "It was business as usual. I was making a pickup and collecting the cash from a sale. It was Giania's family who made the drop. When I approached the car with the cash in the trunk, just as I have done a hundred times, a black man wearing a mask, came out of nowhere and was upon me. Before I knew it I was shot in the chest three times at close range. He took the keys I dropped and left with the car and the two million that was in the trunk."

Nick then said, "While I was lying on the ground, face down, I for whatever reason noticed the man's shoes had four rows of stitching. They were Patton leather shoes, black, and the man who shot me was also black."

I thought to myself it has to be Jerome Attwel from San Francisco. I remember the strange conversation that Nick had with Jerome about his shoes. I told Nick, "If Jerome was here from San Francisco and he was the one who shot you and took the money, the only way he could have known where and when would be is if someone told him. If I am right, that someone would be Steven Besteto." I told Nick, "Stay where you are. **Do not** go anywhere! I will send one of the girls over to stay with you and if you need something let her take care of it."

Nick wanted to know where I was going. I told him, "I am going to go get the money back." Nick said, "I want to go, I want to be part of it." I told Nick, "If you went with me, if you are part of what I am prepared to do, then you would no longer be the same person. Instead you will become the person that I am and you do not want that." I told Nick, "Stay put and leave things to me to handle as I see fit."

After leaving Nick, I went to see big Tony. He was someone I knew I could trust, someone who could help me. Big Tony has always been there for me, though I may not have spoken of big Tony much, he has been a constant in my life for years. After I gave Tony all the details, Tony agreed that it was probably Steven Besteto who set things up. Tony had people in San Francisco that he could trust. He told me I should go to San Francisco. When I got there I was to call the number that he gave me.

Tony said, "Chances are when you get there they will already have picked up Jerome. You can do whatever you need to, but make sure that he tells you everything you need to know before you move on Besteto. Do you understand me?" I told him, "I understand."

I went back to the club, called the airport, and set up a private plane to take me to San Francisco. I left the club via the tunnel to my apartment wearing a disguise, I was headed for the airport.

The next morning I was in San Francisco. When I arrived I called the number Tony gave me. I was told where to go from there. When I arrived, there before me was Jerome Attwel. Tony's people had him tied up, lying on the floor. Jerome had no idea exactly what was going on until he saw me walk into the room.

I told them, "Tie him to a chair." The whole time Jerome was asking, "What is going on? This is a terrible mistake. I have not done anything to you." After they tied him up, I told Jerome, "I want to know who was involved and I want to know where my money is?" Jerome told me that he didn't know what I was talking about. It was then that I reached into the back of my coat and retrieved my knife, the same knife that has served me well throughout the years. I grabbed him by his left ear and in, one stroke, removed it. He screamed!

"Again, who was involved and where is my fucking money?" I told you, "I do not know anything." Jerome screamed at me and again with one stroke the right ear was gone.

I told Jerome, "No matter what, you are a dead man. You tell me what I want and I will end it quick. If not, I am prepared to carve on you until there is nothing left. Again, who was involved and where is my money?"

Jerome told me, "Go fuck yourself." That's was when I then tore his shirt open and cut off both his nipples. Again, he told me, "Go fuck yourself." I reached over and cut off the end of his nose, at that point I noticed that Tony's people where getting a little uneasy.

I told Jerome, "The next thing to go is your testicles." Jerome then decided to start talking, "Ok, I will tell you what you want, just stop. Stop hurting me." I asked, "Who set this whole thing up?"

Jerome told me, "Steven Besteto of Giania family approached me with the whole thing. It was Besteto's idea."

"Where is my money?" Jerome told me, "Besteto has the money. When things cooled off we would meet up at a later date to split the money."

I asked Jerome, "Why not split the money right away with Besteto?" Jerome told me, "After I shot Nick I took the car ten blocks and jumped out. Besteto and his people drove the car into an empty tractor trailer and left with it all. I was given a ride back to the airport and that is all I know."

I grabbed him by his scalp, while still alive, and removed it. He cried in agony and finally, I slit his throat. I let him bleed out, cleaned up, and headed back to Chicago.

The first person I talked to was Big Tony. I told Tony, "Just as I had suspected, Steven Besteto was the one who set the whole thing up."

Tony said, "I know that you are going to kill Besteto and try to retrieve your money, but I want to caution you on how to handle things. Just so we do not end up in an all out battle with Albert Giania."

Tony set a meeting with Albert Giania we told him everything that had happened. I told him, "I am not going to ask your permission to do what I am going to do. I am letting you know this out of respect." Albert Giania said, "I only ask that you do it right away, and that you do it fast because a sharp knife cuts clean and fast with very little mess." I nodded then left the room, leaving Tony and Albert alone. I was headed for Besteto's club the Blue Velvet. This is where I would find him; and my money.

On my way to the club I stopped to check on Nick. When I arrived at Nick's place he seemed to be doing fine. Gina was taking good care of him. Nick wanted to know, "What happened on your trip to San Francisco?" I had to tell him, "Calm down." I believe that he completely forgot about the fact that Gina was still in the room.

I told Gina, "Go put yourself together and leave to go home. Nick is doing fine." After Gina left I told Nick about my trip to San Francisco. I told Nick everything .I thought that Nick would be disgusted by what I had done to Jerome, but just the opposite. Nick told me, "I am glad Jerome is dead and I am happy that he had suffered."

I told Nick, "I am planning on going to the Blue Velvet to confront Steven Besteto." This time, Nick told me, "I am not asking you if I can go, I am telling you that I am going with you."

I told Nick, "Go get dressed; we do not have much time to waste." When we left Nick's place we went to my club. I had some things that I wanted to pick up. Nick and I walked up to the apartment that I kept above the club. I asked Nick to wait in the front room while I go to the back of my apartment. I then went into the tunnel where I kept a variety of weapons and grabbed two M-16 assault rifles. When I came back to where Nick with a duffle bag containing the M-16's and enough ammunition to start a small war. This was exactly what I had in mind.

Nick asked me, "What is in the duffle bag?" I told him, "The duffle bag contains an extreme insurance policy."

We left the club and headed for The Blue Velvet. On the way Nick wanted to know, "What are your plans?" I laughed at him. Nick wanted to know, "What is so funny?" I told him, "I have no real plan other than killing Besteto and hopefully collecting my money." I figured we will wait until the club was closing to make our move."

We parked one blocked from the club. It was maybe forty-five minutes until the club closed. We sat and waited, there was not a great deal of conversation. Twenty minutes before the club closed I spotted Steven Besteto's wife. She pulled up to the front of the club and went inside. I told Nick, "If she is in there when we go in, she is going to meet the same fate as everyone else."

Nick told me, "I thought we were going after Besteto? I did not realize you wanted to kill everyone in the club." I told Nick, "I do not want to kill everyone in the club, but there is no way I am leaving any witness. The only good witness is a dead witness." Nick you need to remember something; I did not ask you to come, you insisted that you come. If you are not prepared to do what needs to be done then you need to stay in the car."

Nick drew a deep breath and said, "I am going in." It was time; we hopped out of the car and opened the trunk. I retrieved an M-16 assault rifle and gave it to Nick, along with plenty of ammunition. I then grabbed my M-16. We hid them under our long winter coats, so that they wouldn't be spotted on our way in.

As we were just about to enter the front door a group of people exited the club. As they walked out, we went in. Just as we entered the club the bartender said, "Hey guys, we are closing in a few minutes." No one recognized us. The entrance to the club was dimly lighted; from where I stood I could see the bartender, one waitress, Besteto, his wife and two of his men.

We started towards the bar, the bartender said, "Are you two stupid, or deaf? We are closing." As I walked by him I drew my pistol which had a silencer on it using my left hand. I kept my right hand on the M-16 rifle. I shot the bartender in the head, as the waitress who was on my right side turned to look at me I shot her in the head.

As we entered the back room Besteto saw me then Nick. He stood up, but before anyone of them could draw their weapons Nick and I drew down on them with our M-16 assault rifles. Something about the sight of a fully loaded M-16 assault rifle brings instant respect because they froze.

Besteto's wife started crying. I told Besteto, "Do something about your wife. Every single one of you put your pistols on the table. There is no point in the two of us having a long drawn out conversation about what you and Jerome Attwell did. Just tell me where my money is."

Besteto asked me, "Would you let my wife go?" I told him, "I cannot do that, but if you give me the money, I will guarantee that she will feel nothing. If you do not give me the money I will take days to kill her and you can watch the whole thing. Now where is my money?" Besteto told me, "It is in the safe in my office."

I told Nick, "Stay here and kill anyone who moves." We walked to Besteto's office. Just as he said, the money was in his safe. He was now trying to negotiate with me, offering more money than he no doubt did not have. We went back to where Nick was holding the rest of them, I told them all, "Walk over and face the wall." Besteto's wife started crying hysterically. Besteto reached over and took her hand. I looked at Nick and nodded, he knew what I wanted. He looked down and shook his head. I leaned over and told him, "If you do not fire your rifle you will stay here with them."

I then sprayed the four of them with fully automatic fire. They all fell and I turned to Nick and told him, "Fire your weapon or die. Remember, you wanted this."

Nick fired his weapon into the already bloody, mutilated, and no doubt dead bodies. I grabbed the money and we left. As Nick and I left we talked somewhat about what had just happened. I told Nick, "I am sorry for the way things went, but my policy is to leave no witnesses. If you did not participate in the killing then you went from an accomplice to witness."

Nick told me, "I understand why you did what you did and I wanted to be here and participate in the revenge that was about to be exacted upon Steven."

It was then that Nick was unable to pull the trigger. Nick told me, "I know I cannot do it." Nick admitted, "I have killed many times while in Vietnam and believed that this would be no different when it came right down to it. When I killed in Vietnam it was for my country, it was for duty, and pride. Killing Besteto, his wife, and everyone else in the club were for revenge,and that's murder."

Nick was unable to cross that line. He told me, "You were right. I am nothing like you and I *don't* want to be like you. I can kill for honor, but I cannot kill for revenge or any other personal emotion." Nick told me, "Your secret is safe with me. I do not want anyone to know what I have been involved in and we shall never speak of what happened again." From that moment on we never spoke of that night again.

Now, with the advantage of hindsight, after that night Nick and I were never the same. I truly believe that night marked the beginning of the end between Nick and me.

The next day all the papers in town carried the news of the killings. The headlines read things like, "The Days of Al Capone are back." Not since the Saint Valentine's Day massacres has Chicago seen mob violence of this nature.

There was a lot of heat coming down on everyone. The police were asking a lot of questions though would never solve the crime. Never the less "Big Tony", Albert, and a number of other people were not happy about the way I handled Besteto. I suppose they were right, I could have waited for a better opportunity to exact my particular brand of justice. With Steven Besteto, as with others in my life, I tended to act extremely violent without the proper amount of thought. When I was in Vietnam they called this a "bullet proof attitude."

I suppose because of all the things I have done and gotten away with I had developed somewhat of a" bullet proof attitude" I didn't care for the heat from the police or the constant thought that one of Steven Besteto's associates might decide to strike at any time.

My normal state of paranoia had become an extraordinary state of paranoia. During this period I rarely left the sanctuary of my club or home. I did frequently visit Cider Falls to see Sarah.

CHAPTER TWENTY-FIVE

It was now June 1979. I was approached by Nick and his boss Terry Nash. They wanted to close "Operation Poppy" down. It would take years to prosecute the hundreds of people involved. Nick and I came up with a plan that would get all of the major players in the same place at the same time.

I contacted all the buyers of the product and told them, "You will have to come to Chicago to the address I give you. It is the address of my house. The reason I am giving the meeting is because I have a new product line that I was to be selling." The new product is cocaine. I let them all know, "You do not have to come, but if you do you will receive first ten kilos of new product free. The next ten will half price."

I had no problems getting everyone to agree on the meeting. Things were set for July 23rd. They will all be at the house by no later than 2:00pm. At exactly 2:15pm the FBI will storm the home and arrest everyone. Things were in place and I suppose I was ready to end the operation. I had amassed a fortune. I had millions and millions of dollars in cash as well as numbered accounts around the world.

Like a bolt of lightning from out of the sky, I received the news that Nick had been killed in a car crash. I wanted to see the body. I found out where the body was being held and when I arrived I asked, "Can I see Nick's body."

The gentlemen in charge asked me, "Were you related?" I told him, "We were brothers." He took me to the room where they store the bodies. It was a cold, uninviting, and dim lighting. It was not a pleasant place, not at all. The gentlemen opened a drawer to reveal a body. The body was concealed under a sheet.

He warned me, "There was a lot of damage to the head. Are you sure you want to proceed?"

I looked at him saying nothing, I just nodded. It was then that he pulled the sheet back slowly, watching me to see if he should stop. I showed no emotion, so he finally pulled the sheet back to reveal Nicks head and upper chest.

If they had not told me that this was Nick I would have had no way to identify him. I asked the gentlemen, "Can you leave me alone for a minute?" He told me, "When you are done, I will be in the other room." When he walked away I stood motionless, just looking. I then reached over grabbed the sheet and pulled it down enough to see Nicks United States Marine Corps tattoo. This must be Nick; the hair was the right color too. Why was I still in a state of disbelief? I then remembered the scar that Nick had at the base of his neck, just under the hair line. This was it, I would look for the scar then I could go home to put this behind me.

In order to satisfy my own paranoia I lifted his head, pulling his hair back, and I looked to where the scar was located. I have seen it a dozen times over the years. Nick told me he got it as a small child when he fell down the steps at his grandmother's house. It was not there, no scar. I looked again, no scar, this was not Nick. Only the government could set up such an elaborate scheme, but why they would go through this trouble?

I was beside myself. What does this have to do with me? Am I on a hit list? The questions were flying at me. This triggered my paranoia. I needed answers and I needed them fast. The only person I know who could possibly help me was Mike Walters, but would he help or was he part of the faking of Nick's death.

It was exactly two weeks to the day from the big meeting at my home was to take place. I spoke to Mike Walters. He seemed to be edgy. I have known him for years and I know when he is acting strange. Mike started by saying, "It is a shame the way Nick had to die." I let Mike talk about Nick's death for a few more moments. I then interrupted Mike by telling him, "Nick is not dead, at least the body I saw was not Nick's."

Mike asked me, "How do you know for a fact that the body you saw was not Nick?" I explained to Mike about the scar at the base of Nick's neck and how the body that I saw had no such scar. It was then that Mike drew a deep breath and cast his eyes downward for a moment before he looked up and made eye contact with me.

Mike told me, "The entire concept of Nick's death was set up and put into motion by the FBI, by Terry Nash. It was believed that the best thing to do was to bring Nick back to keep him safe. By staging Nick's death there would be no one looking for him. It would be easy to keep Nick safe until his testimony was needed." Mike then chuckled, "I suppose no one gave any thought to you figuring out that the body was not his. You have always had a keen eye for details, one small scar at the base of the neck, who would have guessed?" Well Mike, "I need to know where we go from here." Mike replied, "We don't go anywhere. All you have to do is go about business as usual until the meeting. When the day comes the FBI will charge in and bust everyone. After that you will disappear with your millions of dollars and "Operation Poppy" will be effectively shut down."

When I left the meeting with Mike I did not fell completely and totally reinsured by what he told me. I cannot, but help feel that there is more to Nick's death being staged.

For the next week I was extremely cautious about my movements as well as whom I made contact with. I became more reclusive than ever. One week before the big meeting, Mike Walters contacted me. He wanted to meet with me, I told him, "Be at my house by 2:00pm." Mike arrived on time and I could tell there was something he wanted to say because he was acting nervous.

Mike pulled out a pen and paper and wrote on it, your house is bugged. We can't talk here. I motioned for him to follow me. I led him into my office and into the tunnel.

Once we were in the tunnel I told Mike, "You are free to speak." The first thing Mike said was, "What the fuck is this. Where the hell does it go?" I told Mike that it is a tunnel and don't worry about where it goes. Whatever is on your mind just spit it out. "Ok, you want to hear, it then listen up," he said. "Your right about Nick, there is more, much more. I just found out the rest of the story. The FBI on the day of the meeting, during the actual raid itself, plans to assassinate you. Terry Nash himself will lead the raid and one of his cronies will take you out while you supposedly try to escape. Terry Nash figures that since only him, myself, and you, know the whole story behind the heroin ring, the last thing he wants is for you to tell what you know to anyone. He only needs Nick to convict all the people involved. This way they can present Nick as an undercover FBI agent who gained your trust and infiltrated your drug ring. Unfortunately he was never able to find out exactly what your source was."

Mike told me, "The reason I am telling you about your pending assassination is because I owe you on a personal level. As far as I am concerned this evens the score and whatever you do, make sure that you disappear and never surface again." I told him that I would do whatever I had to do when and if the time comes.

After Mike left I knew that I had six days to get my house in order before the meeting. The way my mind works, the first order of business was to make sure Terry Nash was taken care of.

I spent the next six days moving money from numbered accounts to new numbered accounts. I had my lawyer set things up so that the day after the meeting each of my four favorite girls will receive one club each. I left my house, or what would be left of my house, as well as my condominium to my housekeeper. Things were set and before meeting day was over there would be a lot of very surprised people.

My guests started arriving around 1:00pm. By 1:45pm everyone was there. In total there were twenty-six people in the house. Joan had the day off and I insisted that she not come home until after 4:00pm. There was thirty minutes before Terry Nash and the full might of the FBI came crashing in.

I approached Tony and told him, "I needed to talk to you alone." When we entered my den I had only twenty five minutes left. I asked Tony, "Do you trust me?" Tony said, "I do."

"No; Tony, do you trust me with your life. Do you trust me enough to do what I say without question?" Tony asked, "What is up kid?" I again asked "Tony, do you trust me?" "Yes, I trust you," Tony replied. I then opened the door to the den and spoke out in general, "Everyone please make yourself comfortable. Tony and I will be out in fifteen or twenty minutes and then we can begin the meeting." I then returned to the den and looked at Tony. We walked over to the tunnel entrance. When I exposed it to Tony I put my finger to my mouth to let him know not to talk and gestured for him to enter the tunnel. Once in the tunnel I sealed the entrance off. Tony wanted to know, "What in the hell is going on?"

I told Tony, "Not now, we do not have time." We hopped into the golf cart and headed towards the other end of the tunnel and our freedom. Once at the other end we came out of the tunnel and found ourselves in the garage of the other house I owned. We jumped into the car I had in the garage, but before we left I told Tony, "Put on a hat and a pair of sunglasses too."

Tony wanted to know, "What is going on?" He was becoming very adamant about it at this point.

I told Tony, "We have only a few minutes left and there was no time to get into what this was about right now. You only need to believe that I am saving your life. You need to do as I ask, and if you do that everything will be explained in short order."

Tony looked at me and said, "Kid, you better be right." He then put on the hat and sunglasses.

We exited the garage, it's now about twelve minutes past two o'clock. I pulled onto the asphalt, a two lane country road. We drove only a quarter of a mile and I pulled over.

From where I stopped the car I could see the back, the side, and the front of the house. Tony asked, "Now what? Why are we stopping? God damn it kid, your killing me." I replied, "No Tony, just the opposite. I am saving you, just watch."

It was now 2:15pm and from all directions the FBI came charging out of the woods on foot. They came barreling down the driveway; a precession of suburban's all black in color, and then the sound of a helicopter from above. The helicopter landed in the back of the house and the men exited.

Even though we were parked almost one half mile away, I was sure that Terry Nash was one of those men. Tony yelled, "It's the FBI, you knew this was going to happen didn't you?" "Of course I did and that is why we are not down there."

When I was satisfied that Terry Nash was in the house I pulled a remote detonating device from my pocket and pointed it towards the house. When I pushed that button the explosion shook the ground almost half of a mile away. We could feel the blast while we were in the car. Tony's comment was, "Jesus Christ." Tony sat motionless.

What no one knew was that I spent two days placing C-4 explosives throughout the house. I made sure that I placed enough C-4 in the house so that no one would live. The entire house would be reduced to rubble. I have accomplished exactly what I wanted, the house was a pile of rubble, and I later found out that no one in the house lived.

Twenty five of my guests, Terry Nash, and sixteen of his FBI cronies died in that explosion. There were forty-two people in all. "Fuck the FBI." After the explosion we pulled away heading towards Cider Falls. My plan was to drop Tony off in Colorado at the airport. This will give me more than enough time to tell Tony everything now. I said, "Now I will tell you everything. I only ask you do not speak until I am done." I talked non-stop for two hours, telling Tony everything.

In the end, I told Tony, "You have been like a father to me. That is why when we get to Colorado you have to go into the airport with your new identity that I am providing for you. Go to the Dutch West Indies and there you can go to the bank."

I had told him how to access the numbered account that I had set up for him. The account held eight million dollars. It was more than enough to live out his life in comfort and style. I told him, "Look at it like a new lease on life, but understand this Tony. If you decide to go back to the United States you are a dead man. If you contact anyone from your past, they will find you. Do you understand?"

He looked sick, yet he nodded and replied, "I understand. Where are you going kid?" "I am going far away Tony, far away. I suggest that you do the same."

I watched Tony board the airplane and head for the Dutch West Indies. That was the last time I spoke to or ever saw Tony. I found out less than a year later Tony tried to sneak back into the United States. He was captured by the FBI and will, no doubt, spend the rest of his life in prison.

After leaving Tony in that Colorado airport I headed for Cider Falls. I headed straight for Sarah. I headed for what I hoped would be a new chapter in my life, a chapter that would include Sarah, and her son Michael. I now a retired government worker by the name of Mr. Roberts.

CHAPTER TWENTY-SIX

When I arrived in Cider Falls, to the waiting arms of Sarah and the prospect of my new life, it was the most content moment of my life. The look on Sarah's face when I told her, "I am here for good," was priceless. Sarah broke down and started crying, but they were tears of pure joy and happiness. These are the only kind of tears that I ever care to see from Sarah.

Things could not have better; time was going by just fine Sarah's son, Michael and I were getting along great. We seemed to enjoy each other's company. On Michael's tenth birthday, in January, 1980, Sarah took Michael and me aside, away from everyone else. Sarah sat us down and proceeded to tell the both of us, "I have something very important to share with you both."

Sarah looked at Michael and told him, "You are old enough to understand what I am about to say." She said, "To me you need to know the truth. I just hope that neither one of you hate me for what I am about to say." Sarah drew a deep breath before she blurted out, "David, Michael is your son. Michael, David is your father." I could barely speak. My sentences were broken. "You mean? How can it be? I don't understand." Sarah told me, "David, do the math, Michael was born January 1970 you left for Vietnam in May of 1969. When I found out that I was pregnant you were already gone, plus there was that letter you sent me basically telling me that we were finished. I panicked and started dating Daniel. When I came up pregnant he and everyone else assumed that he was the father. I am sorry for not telling the both of you sooner." Sarah started crying I looked at Michael and he looked at me. We both shrugged our shoulders.

I told Sarah, "It is ok. I understand your dilemma. I am not mad, but just the contrary. I am very happy and proud to be Michael's father. If you will let me Michael, I would like to be your new father." It took Michael awhile to respond to what had just taken place. It was probably the longest hardest ten seconds of my life. Sarah and I were both on the edge of our seats waiting for Michael to speak. Then, as if though he had been possessed by greater knowledge and understanding he spoke, *"Cool."*

Sarah and I both looked at each other very strangely. Sarah said, "Cool?" Yeah, Michael said, "Cool." Sara asked him, "So, you are ok with David being your real father." He replied, "Yeah mom, I like David. I am glad I have a father again." Sarah said, *"Cool."*

Michael wanted to know, "Can I go play with my friends now?" Sarah said, "Yes." Sarah and I were both so happy that Michael was alright with everything.

Time passed, the years went by, and life was good. The life I had once lived was a distant memory. Sometimes weeks would go by without me thinking about my past.

Things began to change in 1984. That was the year that Oregon legalized gambling. For whatever reason a gambling interest decided that Cider Falls, and its pristine lake along with the remote wilderness location, would be the perfect place to build a gambling resort.

Throughout the following year properties were being bought at an incredible rate. This was not surprising considering people were being paid twice the market value. By the spring of 1986 the only properties on the lake not bought were Sarah's and mine. It was then that the offers started to become more aggressive.

Until finally in early June 1986, while at the lodge visiting Sarah and I were approached by three men who claimed that they were there on behalf of the Dablanco Gaming Consortium. The one who did all the talking was a middle aged man, well dressed, and well spoken. He started off by telling us, "I have been authorized to offer three times the current value of the properties in order to buy the only two properties left." We both agreed, "The offer was more than substantial, but we are not interested." His mood started to change. He suggested that we take the money because this would be the last and final offer. He then asked me, "How long do you think you will be able to hold up a billion dollar development? The people I represents are growing impatient." He then handed me a card with his phone number. The card read Mr. Carl Alex, Vice-President of Development.

As Mr. Alex was leaving he told the both of us, "I know you two will do the right thing. You have forty-eight hours to change your minds. After that, the offer would be retracted; no matter what it takes I will acquire the properties for DaBlanco Gaming, one way or the other." Then he and his associates got into their car and pulled away. After what he had said to us the hair on the back of my neck stood up. I had an overpowering desire to react violently, but I didn't, I resisted.

That evening, as well as the next day, Sarah and I discussed at great length what we should do. Sarah did not want to sell at any price she wanted to spend her life at the lodge, the only home she has ever known. I on the other hand knew that the DaBlanco Gaming Consortium would stop at nothing to get what they wanted.

Mr. Carl Alex, Vice-President of Development, was in reality nothing more than a high paid gun. He was the muscle that did the dirty work for DaBlanco.

I finally convinced Sarah that in the end we could never win. The best thing to do would be to sell and find some place we liked, a house that we could all live in together. She reluctantly agreed, but I knew that by selling I would be able to keep a low profile, as well as keep Sarah and Michael safe. Men like Mr. Carl Alex do not give up easily.

As we laid in bed that evening we spent hours talking about the sale of our properties. Should we buy or should we build? Sarah and I were both excited about the prospect of starting a new life together. Sharing one home instead of two, Sarah even commented on the possibility of me asking the big question. I laughed and told her, "Anything is possible."

Before we went to sleep we agreed that I would contact Mr. Carl Alex the next day to let him know we will accept the offer. I went to sleep content with what we were doing.

Then it happened. The unspeakable, June 14th, 1986 at three a.m., Sarah and I were awakened by Michael rushing into our room yelling, "The stables are on fire." Before I could stop him he ran out of the room. I told Sarah, "Call the fire department I threw on a pair of pants and chased after Michael.

When I ran up to the stables the fire was completely out of control. I looked franticly for Michael, screaming his name. Where was he? It was then that I caught a glimpse of him through the flames. He was trying to save the horses. I could not get into the stable because of the flames. I screamed at Michael, "Get out of there!" After a few seconds of Michael not responding to my pleas', either because he could not hear me or he was ignoring me, I ran to the opposite side of the stable.

Two horses shot past me, it was then that I heard Michael scream in agony. It was then that the stable collapsed around him. He was gone. There was nothing I could do to save him.

By this time Sarah and all the guests were coming out of the lodge. When Sarah realized that our son Michael perished in the fire, she was inconsolable. In her eyes, the world has just come to an end.

Eventually the fire department arrived and extinguished the fire. The firefighters retrieved what was left of my son, Michael.

The sheriff and the fire chief both, upon being at the scene just a short period of time, felt that the fire was not suspicious in nature. It was most likely caused by faulty wiring. I asked them, "Is that your official findings? To me it seems as if though you two are not even going to bother investigating the fire." The sheriff spoke up right away; I assure you that we will most definitely be doing an investigation, but the initial findings us lead us to believe that it was most likely faulty wiring.

I always thought that the sheriff was on DaBlanco's payroll, now I was convinced, probably the fire chief too. I will deal with all the parties involved when the time was right, but for now I need to be there for Sarah and to put my son to rest.

One week from the day Michael died the official report declared it to be a fire caused by faulty wiring. I did not believe that for one moment. For that very reason I hired myself an outside expert on fire's to review the remains of the stables. His report came back just two days after the official report issued by the fire chief. His report was somewhat different; he concluded that the fire was of a suspicious nature. Most likely arson and it had been done by someone who understood fires. They did a fairly good job of making it seem to be something other than arson.

Now it was a matter of putting things into motion I contacted Mr. Carl Alex and we had a meeting to discuss the sale of the two properties. He was very sympathetic about our loss. Carl offered his condolences.

In the end he paid four times the market value and gave us sixty days to move. We closed the deal ten days later. With money in hand I was able to convince Sarah to find a house to buy quickly and sort things out later. One week after closing she found a house that she liked. We then started the process of moving the contents from the lodge. She wanted the leftovers to be sold at an auction.

Now I faced a very difficult decision. I could forget about my son's death and not punish the men involved or slaughter every remaining soul. I gave careful consideration to my choices, I knew that if I stayed with Sarah the fact that I let the men responsible for Michael's death go unpunished would eat away at me. I also knew that if I did indeed punish those men I would have to disappear and taking Sarah with me was not an option. That would only put the both of us in danger.

I spent the next few weeks moving money from the house and into more off shore accounts. I kept moving the accounts multiple times and I also prepared a series of new identities. It was now time to act.

My first order of business would be the fire chief. I went to his house where he invited me in he was alone and he offered me something to drink I declined. The chief then asked, "How can I help you?" I asked him, "How much?" The chief looked puzzled, "What do you mean, how much?" I again asked, "How much did they pay you to set the fire?" The chief immediately began to deny everything. I then produced a pistol with a silencer and shot him in the leg. The chief fell to the floor yelling, "You have it all wrong. I did not set the fire."

I shot him in the other leg and again asked, "How much?" The chief said, "Please? Please? You do not understand." I then shot him in his foot and again asked the question, "How much?" The chief pleaded with me, "Please stop, just stop. I will tell you everything." I replied, "Start talking." The chief started by telling me that like he said, "I did not set the fire. Mr. Carl Alex had his men did. They told me that no one would get hurt. I am sick about what happened to your son. I can't sleep because my son is the same age. I am *so* sorry."

I asked the chief, "Who approached you?" The chief told me, "I was approached by Mr. Alex and the sheriff. They wanted to know how to set the fire and make it look like an accident."

"How much did they give you?" He told me that they gave him ten thousand dollars. I then looked at the chief and told him, "That was all I needed to know." The chief started begging for his life as I placed three rounds into his chest. I then removed his scalp, a habit I seem to revisit during times of extreme anger or hate. Now it was time to visit the sheriff.

Upon leaving the fire chiefs house I headed straight for the sheriff's. The sheriff only lived a few miles out of town and had no neighbors within a mile. His house could not be seen from the road.

I pulled down the driveway right up to the house, and when I approached the front door the sheriff's wife walked out and asked, "Can I help you?" I told her, "I would like to talk to the sheriff if he is available." She told me, "He is out back in the shed where he spends most of his time. His hobby is wood crafting." She then offered her condolences for the death of my son. She turned and re-entered the house.

Unfortunately for her she was a witness, something I would not need. I placed two shots into the back of her head using a pistol with a silencer.

I then made my way to the sheriff's shed. When I went into the shed sure enough there was the sheriff working on some sort of wood project. I stood motionless for several minutes watching the sheriff working. When he turned off the tool he was working with and turned around he finally noticed me.

The sheriff claimed, "You startled me. Can I help you Mr. Roberts?" I started off slow. I told him, "To begin with you can tell me what you know about my son's death." The sheriff told me, "Your son died in a tragic accident to which no one was at fault. You should quit looking for something that is not there. You should be there for Sarah and stay strong."

It was then that I produced my pistol. The sheriff immediately made it clear to me that I should put the pistol away and go home before I ended up in serious trouble. Besides he said, "You are not the type who could harm someone."

It was then that I shot him in the groin. He collapsed to the ground. I informed him, "I could not only kill you, but I will be sending you to hell for what you did. Someday I will be seeing you there because hell is where I am headed." I then finished him off with two shots to the head. Once again I took a trophy, his scalp.

I then decided to get back to Sarah. As far as Sarah was concerned I had been at the lake house packing for the big move.

The next day, late that afternoon, Sarah came to me to tell me about what she had heard while in town. Sarah could not believe what had happened to the fire chief, the sheriff, and to the sheriff's wife. "Why would someone do this? How could someone do this?"

I told Sarah, "I do not know why or who could do such a thing, but in light of what had happened, I feel best if you went to Idaho to visit her aunt for a few days. Just until they catch the person responsible."

It took some convincing, but she agreed to leave the next day. When Sarah left I knew it was probably the last time I would see her, but I also knew it was for the best. The evening after she left would be the evening that I would exact justice on Mr. Carl Alex and his henchmen. Mr. Alex has taken up residence in one of the homes across the lake that has not been demoed yet for the impending casino and hotel construction.

I decided that the best way to approach the house was to come across the lake at night, there was a quarter moon that night so I had enough light. I took a chance going around the lake, following the shore. I was staying only a couple hundred feet away from shore, but yet it was far enough away as not to be detected.

I arrived at the house around one a.m. I took my time getting to the house, carefully watching as I circled the house. While looking in the windows I spotted Mr. Alex. He was sitting at a desk talking on the phone with someone. I could over hear what he was saying. Apparently the person on the other end was his boss at DaBlanco's. Mr. Alex told him, "You are just as guilty as I am when it comes to the death of that boy."

I stood quietly and silently watching and listening Mr. Alex continued to talk on the phone. I heard him say, "The boys and I are coming back to Los Angeles until the police find whoever it is that's doing the killing. I already told you who I think it probably is and like I said, you're just as guilty as I am." The conversation ended abruptly after that comment, Mr. Carl Alex seemed very agitated. I then heard Mr. Alex call out, "Come on you guys. Let's get out of here."

I took this as my queue to make my move. I walked around to the front of the house, where one of the men was loading luggage into the car. He had left the front door of the house slightly opened. While he was preoccupied with loading the trunk of the car I managed to slip into the house unseen. Mr. Alex was still seated at the desk, his back turned to me.

The third man was still upstairs; I could hear him shuffling about. I had a pistol tucked into my pants and in my hands I held a sawed off double barreled, twelve gauge shot gun. Mr. Alex did not know I was in the room until I placed the shot gun to the base of his head. I told him, "Do not move or do anything foolish. Call your men into the room and remember both barrels are going to be pointed at you."

I then concealed myself behind the door. Mr. Alex stood facing the door. As the two men entered I took my foot and pushed the door shutting it behind them. I told everybody, "Do not move. Put your weapons on the desk and lay down on the floor one at a time." I had Mr. Alex take the phone cords and tie the two men's hands' behind their backs.

After that I had Mr. Alex remove his shirt which I used to tie his hands behind his back. At that point I had all three men lying on the floor face down. I pulled their pants down around their ankles. They would not be able to use their legs now. After I was comfortable with that fact that they had been rendered harmless I left the room and went thru the house, gathering all the phone cords I could find. I returned to the room where Mr. Alex and his two associates where lying. I took the phone cords that I had gathered and used them to tie their hands to their legs, this brought back memories of my childhood on the farm. I had hog tied them as my father taught me. There they were, the three of them lying on their stomachs, face down, legs bent up, and tied to their hands which were tied behind their backs. *They were a pitiful sight!*

Now I could relax, I could extract whatever information from them that I wanted. I pulled a chair over to where they were sitting. I started by asking Mr. Alex, "Who have you been talking to?" He told me, I have not been talking to anyone and I want to know why you are here." I told him, "I have already dealt with the fire chief and the sheriff. Now it was time to deal with the three of you. If you answer my questions truthfully I will make your deaths quick. If you do not answer my questions honestly I will kill each of you slowly, piece by piece."

Mr. Alex began to plead, as most men do when faced with their own deaths, "Mr. Robert your son's death was an accident. No one was supposed to get hurt. We were just supposed to send you a message. We can work something out. The people I work for have a great deal of money."

I told him, "I will only ask one more time, who were you talking to on the phone?" Mr. Alex started by saying, "Mr. Roberts, please be reasonable." It was then that I knew he did not seem to understand how this question and answer session was supposed to work. So, I resorted to tactics that had worked for me in the past. I reached down and cut off his right ear. "Once again, Mr. Alex, who were you talking to?" Once he composed himself and told me, "I was on the phone with Richard Martins."

"Alright Mr. Alex, now we are making progress. Is he the one who told you to send me a message?"

"Yes, Mr. Richard Martins is the one who told me to send you and Sarah a message."

"Where can I find Martins?"

"He is the President of Operations at DaBlanco Gaming."

"Where is his office located?"

"His office is located in Los Angeles, at DaBlanco Gaming Headquarters."

"Alright, Mr. Alex I appreciate your honesty, so as promised I will make your death quick." They were whimpering, waiting for me to shoot them I suppose, but shooting them would have been doing them a favor. My son burned, so they can burn too. I walked thru the house starting spot fires. It was not long before they figured out what I was doing Mr. Alex was yelling, "You promised us you would make it quick." I walked back to where I had them tied up and told them, "To me, this was a quick death, and it's more than you disserve?" I walked out of the house and stood there for almost ten minutes. During that time I could hear the three of them screaming and yelling in terror and pain. All I felt was satisfaction; *"Fuck them."*

When the house was fully engulfed in flames I went back to my canoe and made my way back to my lake house. All the way back to the lake house I could look over my shoulder and see the fire light up the sky. When I arrived at my house all I needed to do was to collect a few things from my desk and get into my car, which was already packed, and head to Los Angeles to find Mr. Richard Martins.

I went into my den, where I kept my desk, to collect some paperwork that I needed. While sitting at the desk looking through some paperwork I heard a voice from the past. It was Mike Walters, "Don't move and put your hands where I can see them." The sound of his voice along with what he said sent chills down my spine. Mike was not there to talk about old times. He was there to kill me. I lifted my head slowly and then put my hands on top of the desk. After Mike was satisfied he stepped out of the shadows, "Hello Cavanaro. I suppose you know why I am here."

I told him, "Yes, I suppose I know why you are here." Mike, how did you find me?"

"When I heard that a fire chief and a sheriff had been killed and scalped I knew it was you. In my entire life I have never known of, nor had he ever heard of, anyone who scalps their victims. In my opinion it was for whatever reason something that has stuck with you since Vietnam and once I knew your general location, finding you would not be too hard."

I looked at Mike and smiled I told him, "Just as we have discussed in the past, people are creatures of habit. In this case my one bad habit, my one tell tale sign, may cost me my life." Mike said, "No Cavanaro, not that it may cost you your life, but it *will* cost you your life."

By the look on his face I knew that the moment was near. Mike, I suppose that I don't have any credit left with you do I?"

"No, you don't. You used up all your credit in Chicago. You couldn't just leave quietly. You couldn't just disappear and leave Terry Nash alone. No matter how many people you had to kill you just had to get even, and at any rate you know way too much."

It was then; right then that Mike's eyes squinted, his muscles tensed up, and his arm straighten out. He was getting ready to pull the trigger and nothing I could say would stop him. At least that is what Mike Walters thought, what Mike did not know is I had installed a double barrel sawed off twelve gauge shotgun to the underside of the desk, connected by wires, and pulleys to a foot pedal. At the exact moment that I was sure Mike was going to pull the trigger I took my right foot and stepped on the pedal. Both barrels fired at the same time.

The explosion was almost deafening. The front of the desk exploded, throwing Mike across the room. I ran from around the desk and kicked his pistol to the side. The bulk of the shotgun blast hit Mike in the lower abdomen. He had large wood splinters embedded in his abdomen, legs, and chest. I looked at Mike and told him, "I am sorry you found me."

He could not say much, but what he did say was, "I did not see that coming." He then died. I finished what I had been doing and set the house on fire. I hopped into my car and headed for Los Angeles.

Forty miles down the road I stopped to switch vehicles. I stashed a car two days earlier that I purchased under a different name.

Later the next day I was in Los Angeles, now to locate Richard Martins. Upon arriving in Los Angeles I found myself a place to stay. I felt that a hotel would be risky because if someone was not looking for me it would not be long before they were. With that in mind I rented a small, off the beaten path, apartment. Once I was settled in I started my hunt, and hunting is exactly what I was doing.

It was not hard to located DaBalanco's Headquarters, but locating Richard Martins would prove to be slightly more difficult. After two days of watching and waiting I was becoming inpatient. On day three I decided to use a different approach I changed my appearance to that of an older man, in my sixties.

With my new look in place I walked into the lobby of DaBlanco's office building. I walked to the information board and found Richard Martins name and office number. I walked onto the elevator and went to the twenty-second floor, room 2216. When I entered the room I was greeted by Mr. Martin's secretary, I asked her, "Is Mr. Martins in? If so, may I please speak to him?"

She spoke in a very soft, but professional voice, "Mr. Martins is not in. Is there something I could do for you?" No Nancy, I hope you don't mind me calling you Nancy, after all your name is on your desk."

"No I don't mind," she replied. Well Nancy, though I do appreciate your offer, my business is with Mr. Martins. Do you expect him back soon?" No, I do not," Nancy replied. She then went on to tell me, "Mr. Martins has taken off work for personal reasons and I am really not sure when he will be back." I thanked her for her help and I left the building.

I knew that a man like Mr. Richard Martins did not make a move without his personal secretary having firsthand knowledge of what he was doing or where she could contact him. I waited for Nancy to get off work. When she left the parking garage I was not far behind. I followed her, waiting for her to possibly make a stop. If necessary I would follow her to her home.

It turned out that I was fortunate enough to have her stop at the grocery store. While she was shopping I positioned my car close to hers. After twenty minutes or so she exited the store. I took this opportunity to accidentally bump into her when she was just a few feet from her car. I walked right past her and she glanced at me I blurted out, "Nancy is that you?" Nancy replied, "I thought I recognized you." We exchanged pleasantries for a few moments and I informed her, "My car had just broken down. I am going to be late for my granddaughters' birthday party and I am trying to find a phone so I can get a ride. I will tend to the car tomorrow."

Nancy asked, "Where are you going exactly?" Maybe I can give you a ride."

I responded by asking her, "Which way are you going?" She told me, "The direction she was headed and I told her, "You can drop me off on your way if you did not mind." Nancy said, "That would not be a problem." I helped her finish loading her groceries and before I knew it I was in her car. Before we exited the parking lot Nancy wanted to know, "Exactly; what do you want to be dropped off?"

Once we were on the main road I made my true extensions known to her. At first Nancy started to panic, but I quickly assured her, "If you do what I ask of you then you will not be harmed. All I want to know is where is your boss Mr. Martins?"

At first she insisted, "I do not know. He left town suddenly on personal business."

I assured her, "I know you are not telling me the truth and if you insist on lying to me that I am prepared to get the information from you. This means by anyway I have to."

In a very short time Nancy decided to quit lying. She told me where her boss was. It seemed he was only a few hours away. He was staying at a beach house owned by the Delanco Corporation I thanked Nancy for the information and told her to drive me to the beach house. She did not argue with me, she just drove.

We passed the time with idle chit chat, nothing to serious. I was trying to keep her calm and she was doing likewise. Just as Nancy had told me, after a few hours we had arrived at the beach house.

The beach house was located in a somewhat secluded area, which meant I more that likely would not be noticed approaching the house. I had Nancy drive the car a quarter of a mile down the road where there was a place to park the car. I took Nancy to the back of the car and opened the trunk. With a sweater that I took from the back seat and cut into strips I tied her legs and her arms behind her back. Just before I gagged her, so that she could not scream I asked her, "Is your boss alone?"

Before she could answer I told her, "If you lie to me when I return I will kill you, but if you tell me the truth you would live."

Nancy told me, "My boss is not alone; he has two armed body guards with him."

As I was starting to gage her she turned her head and said, "There is something I have to know. Are you him? Are you Mr. Roberts from Cider Falls, Oregon?" I told her, *"I am!"*

She told me, "I do not know how that was possible because Mr. Roberts was a much younger man."

I looked at her and told her, "Things are not always as they appear." I then gagged her and shut the trunk.

Now to finish what I had started as I made my way down to the beach towards the house. I could see the lights from the house getting closer and closer. Finally, I was so close to the house that from my vantage point I could now see inside.

Now to wait and watch, I was waiting for some sign of life, some sort of movement, some idea of where the people inside were located so that I could decide what method of approach would work best.

I then saw one of the men walk out of the house, onto the terrace, and light a cigarette. He then walked down the steps, onto the beach, and stood there for a moment. He then turned towards the direction in which I was hiding and headed straight at me.

I concealed myself behind a small outcropping of rocks. I was not sure whether or not he would come to my exact location or stop short. I stood quietly waiting. He actually walked right past me. We were within ten feet of each other and he had no idea that he was not alone on that beach.

As he passed me I stepped out from my hiding place and with my pistol in hand I pointed it directly at his head and I told him, "Lie face down on the beach." I then relived him of his weapon and I let him get up.

Before, either one of us could speak, a second man came out of the house onto to the terrace and hollered, "Joe, where are you at?"

I looked at Joe and told him, "Answer him."

Joe yelled back, "I am over here."

The other man hollered back, "Come on. Dinner is almost ready."

Once again Joe answered by yelling, "Alright. I'll be there in a minute."

I told Joe, "It is your choice, you can live or die, and all I want is your boss Mr. Martins. If you do as I say you can live."

Joe, as most people, chose life. Joe and I headed towards the beach house, towards the terrace, and the conclusion of what I had came here for. Once on the terrace, at the back door, I could see Mr. Martins. He was seated at the kitchen table; the other body guard was standing at the stove.

I told Joe, "Open the door. Let's go in."

As we entered Mr. Martins saw that Joe was not alone. The other body guard turned and when he saw me out of instinct he reached for his gun. I then pushed Joe away from me, turned, and shot the body guard at the stove. He was dead instantly.

Mr. Martins was still seated it was as if he were frozen. I turned to Joe and simply said, "You picked the wrong career and I shot him." Now it was just I and Mr. Richard Martins. Still Mr. Martins sat there in that chair frozen in place. I told him, "I suppose you know why I am here." He asked, "Are you Mr. Roberts?"

I told him, "I am."

He told me, "I am sorry for what happened to your son. No one was supposed to get hurt. I wish I could take it all back. Killing me will not bring your son back." He then offered me money.

I told him, "People like you, people with power and money, always believe you can buy your way out of everything. However you are right about one thing. Killing you will not bring my son back, but then not killing you will not bring my son back either."

He then told me, I will go to the police and I will confess everything."

This sparked an idea in my mind. I told him, "You won't contact the police, but what you are going to do is call the FBI office in Los Angeles and you will confess everything to them. You will do it in three minutes or less. I do not want you staying on the phone for fifteen, twenty or thirty minutes. You will make it short and fast then maybe, just maybe, I won't kill you."

Mr. Martins stood up, went to the telephone in the other room, and called the operator. He had her put him in touch with the FBI office in Los Angeles.

I told him, "When you are finished, before you hang up the phone, tell them that my name is not Mr. Roberts. That my name is David Michael Cavanaro, a name they will be familiar with." When the FBI answered the phone Mr. Martins began talking. He talked uninterrupted and told the story of my son's death. He then told them my true name or least a name they would no doubt recognize. He then hung the phone up and after that he immediately began begging for his life.

I knew that he was not the man who set the fire, and I knew that he did not tell anyone else to harm my son. In the end people like Mr. Martins, people with power and money, people at the top, set the policies that allow this sort of behavior. They almost always remain in the shadows and allow other people to take the fall. Well this must have been Mr. Martins' lucky day because I would allow him to live.

I took Mr. Martins back into the kitchen and sat him in a chair. I then tied him to the chair using phone cords and I told him, "I have decided you will live." I then took out my knife, the same knife I have had all these years, and removed his scalp. Then I sliced both his eyes, leaving him blind for life.

The entire time he was screaming in obvious pain. When I was leaving the house I took his scalp and pinned it to the kitchen wall. I then went back to the car and let Nancy out of the trunk. I told her, "Just as I promised, I will not harm you".

I had her drive me back to Los Angeles. Along the way Nancy asked me, "What did you do to my boss Mr. Martins?"

I told her, "Do not concern yourself with Mr. Martins. You will be best served to concentrate on the drive back to Los Angeles and your own welfare. Whatever had happened, or not happened to Mr. Martins does not concern you nor does discussing it change anything."

We went for the most part of the drive back to Los Angeles not speaking. When we arrived in town I had her take me to a busy part of the city. She pulled the car over and before I exited the car I told Nancy, "I am genuinely sorry for what I have put you through. Unfortunately for you I knew that I could get to your boss through you. When I get out of your car you just drive away, do not stop, and just drive." I then exited the car and Nancy drove away. I disappeared into the crowd. Disappearing is easy it was being ordinary that was the key to remaining unnoticed. It is the key to being just another face in the crowd and when you put that together with almost unlimited money, the ability to acquire different identities, the ability to change your appearance, you can be almost anybody you want.

CHAPTER TWENTY-SEVEN

Here I am today, just another face in the crowd. Out there, somewhere just beyond reach. It has been five years since I have spoken to Sarah. I have seen her twice even though she does not know it. I know that I can have no direct contact with her, but I still like to look in on her from time to time. For the most part my life has become serene, almost peaceful. If you are wondering what would prompt me to take pen in hand to tell the story of my life, I suppose it was the realization that they will *never* stop looking for me.

Just one year ago in London I was being watched. My movements were being tracked and there were two men in a car following me. I pulled over, parked the car, and went into a shop. I found my way out of the shop thru the rear door and worked my way around the car where the two men were parked.

There was no doubt that they were following me. I was close enough to see that the back door of the car was unlocked I simply jumped into the back seat of the car and I had dropped both of them.

I asked them, "What do you want?"

Well, just as I thought they were CIA agents. They had been watching me for two days and they wanted to make sure they had the right person before they acted. That was their mistake, I killed both of them and I once again disappeared.

It was then I decided to write my life story. I have sent a copy of my writings to all the major news papers of the United States and abroad. Each person receiving this information will also receive a portion of the human ears I have taken throughout my life. One of you will receive the cape that I have fashioned of human scalps.

The majority of the information within these pages will be easy to verify. Everything I have written is true. I have not embellished the facts because they need not be embellished. I am a real person and this is my life. I am out there somewhere, someplace, and let this be a warning to those who may try to find me. Be careful of that which you wish for, for what you wish for may not be what you want. Strike fast, strike first, and strike without mercy, for if you do not, *I most assuredly will.*